SPECIAL MESSAGE TO READERS

SPLINTERED CANYON

The Splintered Canyon Bunch is out to kill Frank Slessor! Luckily, his old friend Jet Barclay finds him first, persuading Slessor to accompany him to Wind Creek and assist in its sorely-needed pacification. En route, they discover that Ral Craven, the outlaw leader, is attempting to take over the local cattle shipment business in the town of Poverty. As events spiral and lead flies, the Splintered Canyon Bunch seems to hold all the cards — but who will win the final hand?

EMMETT STONE

SPLINTERED CANYON

Complete and Unabridged

LINFORD
Leicester

First published in Great Britain in 2013 by
Robert Hale Limited
London

First Linford Edition
published 2015
by arrangement with
Robert Hale Limited
London

A catalogue record for this book is available
from the British Library.

ISBN 978–1–4448–2394–3

Published by
F. A. Thorpe (Publishing)
Anstey, Leicestershire
Set by Words & Graphics Ltd.
Anstey, Leicestershire
Printed and bound in Great Britain by
T. J. International Ltd., Padstow, Cornwall

This book is printed on acid-free paper

1

Barclay spent some time looking for the Grand Regal Hotel, but he couldn't find it. There were two others — the Redwing and the Franklin. He checked both of them out but there was nothing in the hotel register and the clerk in each case did not recognize Barclay's description of his friend. It was only by chance that he came across the place he was looking for. The broken-down sign read *Palace Lodgings* but a less appropriate title it would have been hard to imagine. The place was a flop-house.

He had almost passed it by when, on a whim, he stopped in his tracks, turned and went through the entrance. It was dark inside and the place smelt of stale vegetables and tobacco. There were several doors and he knocked on two of them without success. The third time the door opened and a scrawny old woman in a nightdress peered out at him.

'Sorry to disturb you, ma'am,' he said. 'I'm lookin' for a man named Slessor. He'd be about my age but taller. The distinctive thing about him is that he has the tip of an ear missing.'

'The right ear?' the old woman said.

'Nope, the left, but I figure the details don't matter.'

The woman thought for a moment, her mouth twisting into an indeterminate slash. 'Try the next floor, second on the right. I don't know if he'll still be there. Ain't seen him just recently.'

'Thank you, ma'am,' Barclay replied. He touched his hand to the brim of his Stetson. He turned and made his way to the foot of the stairway, where he paused to glance back. The woman was standing in the doorway watching him. He nodded and she went back inside, closing the door softly behind her. He began to mount the stairs. Faded wallpaper barely clung to the damp, stained walls. The stairs creaked and there were holes in the treads. Above him the stairwell was a pit of darkness. Without thinking, he drew his Smith & Wesson No. 3 revolver from its holster.

He reached the top of the stairs and turned to the right. The woman had said the second on the right. He stepped across and put his ear to the door but there was no sound from within. He bent down and looked through the keyhole. A cold draught seemed to blow into his eye. He stood up straight and knocked on the door. There was no response. He knocked again. He waited for a moment, listening carefully, but the only sound was the drip of water coming from somewhere further along the corridor. He thought for a moment or two and then, taking a step back, he swung his leg and brought his boot slamming into the door. To his surprise it flew open. Holding his gun out in front of him, he burst into the room.

The room was dark but his eyes

quickly adjusted. It was bare. The only items of furniture were a chair, a table and a bed frame on which lay a figure with its head against the wall. Whoever it was, he showed no sign of interest. For a moment Barclay wondered if he was dead. He moved forward till he was standing over the foot of the bed. The man wasn't dead. He lay still, not moving a muscle, but his eyes were open and he was staring fixedly at the newcomer. Barclay breathed a sigh of relief. The old woman was right. The man on the bed was his old partner, Frank Slessor.

'Slessor!' he said. 'I've been lookin' for you.' The man did not respond immediately but after a moment Barclay thought he detected a spark of interest pass across his sharply etched features.

'Barclay?' he said. 'Jet Barclay? That was quite an entrance.'

Barclay glanced around the dingy room. 'The door wasn't locked,' he replied. 'Isn't that a bit careless?'

'I figure you're the careless one,' Slessor replied. 'You were outlined against that door frame. You're lucky I didn't shoot you.'

Barclay's gaze returned to the recumbent figure. His hands lay loosely across his chest. 'You ain't carryin' a gun,' he said. 'You must be feelin' confident.' He holstered his weapon and walked to the window, across which a tattered curtain was drawn. He pulled it aside and shreds of fading afternoon sunlight entered the room. He turned back. Slessor had swung himself off the worn mattress on which he had been lying and was running his fingers through his tangled hair.

'Hell, this place gives me the creeps,' Barclay said. 'Why don't we take a walk over to the nearest saloon?'

Slessor nodded. 'That's OK with me,' he said, 'only, you might have to pay.' He walked across to the table and opened a drawer. Out of it he pulled a gun, which he thrust into his belt. 'I'm carryin' a gun now,' he said. Barclay

5

didn't inquire if his change of mind was an indication that he thought he might need it.

Barclay felt his spirits lift as soon as they emerged from the flop-house. Together, he and Slessor made their way to the next junction where a short walk brought them to the Silver Spur on Main Street. Before they stepped up to the boardwalk, Slessor looked at the horses which were tethered outside.

'Lookin' for somethin'?' Barclay asked.

'Nope. Guess it's just an old habit.'

Barclay didn't reply. Slessor rejoined him and they stepped through the batwings. At that hour, the place was relatively quiet but taking a look around at some of the clientele, Barclay had a feeling that it might get pretty rowdy later. A girl approached them as they crossed the smoke-laden room but Barclay brushed her aside.

'Take a seat,' he said to Slessor. 'I'll be right back.'

He ordered a bottle of bourbon and a

couple of glasses. When he looked for Slessor, he saw that he had taken a table in a corner, which gave him a good view of the room and protected his back. Another one of Slessor's old habits. He took a seat and poured the whiskey.

'You'll pardon me for sayin' it,' he remarked as they raised their glasses, 'but you look as though you could do with this.'

Slessor tossed the glass back, then gave Barclay a searching look. Barclay wasn't sure whether it was due to the whiskey, but it seemed to him that Slessor was already looking more animated.

'It was obviously no accident that you found me,' he said. 'I reckon you'd better tell me what you're doin' in Ghost Hill.'

Barclay poured each of them another glass. 'Yeah. But I think you got some explainin' to do, too.'

Slessor was about to reply when the batwings flew open and four men burst into the room. His eyes followed them as they strode to the bar, their boots and spurs making a lot of noise in the process. 'Before either of us starts,' he said quietly to Barclay, 'I figure you'd better either leave right now or get ready for trouble.'

The men at the bar were talking and laughing loudly with a couple of the girls. They weren't taking much notice of anybody else and hadn't glanced in the direction of the corner where Barclay and Slessor were sitting.

'You mean those boys at the bar?' Barclay replied. 'You know them?'

'No, but I reckon they'll know me when they see me.' He suddenly looked serious. 'Those boys are lookin' for me, but it ain't none of your business. I don't want — '

'I'm stayin',' Barclay interrupted. He couldn't be certain, but he thought he detected the hint of a grin on Slessor's face. He recalled what had happened earlier that day. 'You were waitin' for them back at the flop-house,' he said.

'But the door was open and your gun was in the drawer. I don't understand.'

Slessor took another drink of whiskey. 'Let's just say things have already changed since then,' he said.

Barclay was about to ask another question but he didn't get the chance. Suddenly there was a commotion at the bar and above the hubbub a voice rang out.

'Say, ain't that Slessor sittin' at the table over in the corner?'

Barclay and Slessor were suddenly the centre of attention. A piano had been playing in a desultory sort of way but the notes trailed away and then stopped. Conversation was stilled as a hush descended. Although he had his back to the bar, Barclay was aware that the four newcomers were staring at them. In a few moments he heard the sound of boots stamping across the floor. Slessor had finished his second drink and his hand was on the bottle as he poured himself another. The footsteps stopped and a voice rasped out.

'Slessor, this is a surprise. We didn't figure to find you so easily.'

Slessor did not reply. Barclay turned in his chair to look up into the ugly face of the speaker. He recognized the type; all four of them bore the unmistakable stamp of hired killers, of men who made a living by the gun.

'You, git!' the man rapped, addressing Barclay.

Barclay continued to look into his face a moment longer before turning to Slessor. 'You know this *hombre?*' he said. 'Seems to me he's a mite unfriendly.'

'You got just this one chance to get out of here,' the man said.

'I ain't finished my drink,' Barclay replied.

The man turned to his companions with an ugly leer. 'What do you think, boys? Do we let him finish his drink?'

The other three grinned and one of them let out a sneering laugh. Barclay glanced swiftly at Slessor. He knew what was coming and he knew which of

10

the gunmen to go for. In a moment the years fell away and the old rapport was as fresh as ever.

Without warning, all four of the gunnies went for their shooters but before they had come free of leather, Slessor's gun had sent the two opposite him reeling back while Barclay's poured hot lead into the others, including the man who had been doing the talking. Slessor leaped to his feet, sending the table crashing to the floor as he did so. As a couple of the gunnies returned fire, both he and Barclay ducked behind it. Shards of wood went flying into the air but neither gunman got the chance to fire again as bullets from Barclay's Smith & Wesson found their targets.

One of the other gunmen lay slumped against the bar, unmoving, but the man who had spoken was attempting to crawl away, dragging his leg behind him. Springing from cover, Slessor raced over to him and stamped down hard on his injured limb. The man gave a howl of pain and then lay whimpering.

'Where are the rest of 'em?' Slessor snapped. The only reply was a groan and Slessor bent down, seized the man by the collar and dragged him screaming to his feet.

'I asked a question. Where are the others?'

'They're at the Green River Tradin' Post.'

Slessor held him up for a moment longer before allowing him to slump back to the ground.

'I need a doc,' the man moaned. 'Get me a doc.'

Just at that moment the batwings swung open and a tall man with greying hair came into the room. He looked about him, taking in the scene. He glanced at the whining figure of the gunman and then at Slessor.

'Ask any of these folks,' Slessor said. 'They'll tell you what happened. We didn't start it.'

The saloon began to come back to life. 'Like he says, it was self-defence,' someone said and a few other voices took up the theme. The marshal strode to the bar where he spoke with the barman. While they were talking, Barclay, having checked that the other gunnies were dead, joined Slessor. In a few moments the marshal came back.

'Seems like you're tellin' the truth,' he said. 'All the same, I want the two of you out of town by dawn tomorrow.'

Barclay and Slessor exchanged glances. 'Sure,' Barclay said. 'We weren't figurin' to stay around Ghost Hill anyway.'

'What about him?' Slessor said, nodding at the prostrate form of the injured gunslinger.

'Leave him to me. I'll take him over to the jailhouse.'

Slessor seemed about to add something but Barclay took him by the arm and led him towards the batwings. Before they could exit the marshal shouted after them.

'Forget what I just said. I may need to talk to you boys about this. Where can I find you?'

'At the Franklin Hotel,' Barclay replied.

Slessor gave him a curious look but Barclay ignored it. He gave Slessor a push and together they stepped through the batwings into the street. It was growing dark. Scattered lights were beginning to appear along the main drag.

'You got a horse?' Barclay asked.

'I did have,' Slessor replied.

'Never mind. We can pick up mine from the livery and buy or hire one for you.'

Slessor stopped in his tracks. 'You seem in a mighty hurry to get away,' he said.

'I don't trust the marshal not to change his mind. I know that fight wasn't any of our askin' and the marshal seems to agree, but all the same we might have ended up in jail. At the very least things could get complicated. I take it you haven't got any reason to stay in town?'

Slessor laughed. 'You ain't wrong there,' he said.

'Right. Then let's get out of here

14

while we can.' Barclay looked at his companion. 'I still haven't got round to tellin' you yet what I'm doin' in Ghost Hill and I figure you've got more explainin' to do than I thought.' They turned a corner. The livery stable was just a little way ahead.

'Just one thing?' Slessor said.

'Yeah, I know,' Barclay replied. 'Whatever else we decide, you want to pay a visit to the Green River Tradin' Post. Well, I guess we'll be needin' some supplies and I suppose that's as good a place as any to pick them up.'

* * *

After collecting the horses, they rode at a steady pace till darkness had descended. A big orange moon swam into the sky and they found a place to make camp. Barclay felt strangely exhilarated and it seemed to him that Slessor was feeling something of the same. Already he appeared to be a different man from the one he had found in the sordid hotel room. By the time they had eaten and drunk a couple of cups of coffee, they were in a relaxed and comfortable frame of mind. Barclay got out his pack of Bull Durham, took some tobacco and a paper and handed the pack to Slessor.

'OK,' he said, 'I figure you got the most explainin' to do.'

'Yeah. I suppose you're wonderin' what that was all about back at the Silver Spur?'

'That, and just what you were doin' lyin' around that hotel room with the door open. Especially if you had a notion that those gunhawks were around.'

Slessor leaned forward and took a pull on the cigarette he had built. He drew the smoke deep into his lungs. 'Ain't had a good smoke in a whiles,' he commented. Barclay remained silent, waiting for Slessor's explanation.

'I knew those gunnies were coming for me,' Slessor said. 'Maybe not just those ones we had the fight with, but others just like them. I knew they were comin' but somehow it didn't seem to matter.'

'Didn't seem to matter!' Barclay expostulated.

'Things haven't been goin' so well for me recently. I guess I was just down on my luck.'

'What had you done to upset them?' Barclay asked.

'You remember the Splintered Canyon Bunch?'

'Sure. They caused a whole heap of trouble down along the Rio Grande till the law finally caught up with them. They were led by two brothers. One of them got shot and the other got put behind bars.'

'Yeah. Well that was my doin'. I'm the man who shot Johnny Craven and sent Ral Craven to the penitentiary.'

'That was some time ago.'

'Long enough for Ral to have served his time. Seems like he's out of jail and formed a new gang. Now he's lookin' for revenge. Somehow, he musta found

out where I was. I noticed I was bein'
followed. I caught up with a couple of
the varmints tailin' me and squeezed
the information out of them. I moved
on. The same thing happened. Then,
like I say, I hit some hard times. When I
realized they were back on my trail, I'd
already decided that I'd had about
enough. It didn't seem worth makin'
the effort any more. I figured, why not
let Ral have his revenge? He'd be doin'
me a favour. But there was another
thing. I had a kinda hunch that Craven
would want me alive. He's just the sort
of evil son of a gun who'd want to
savour his revenge and drag it out real
slow.'

'You seem to have changed your
mind fairly quickly.'

'I guess, after all, feelin' that way was
only a phase. When the door to the
hotel room bust open, I figured Ral's
gunnies had found me. When I saw it
was you, somethin' happened. I don't
know; it was like some kinda sign.'

'I can't have got there much ahead of

them. It was a close call.'

'Yeah. Now, you haven't said what you were doin' in Ghost Hill. I reckon it's your turn to talk.'

Barclay paused for a moment before leaning his head back against his saddle and drawing in the smoke from his cigarette. He looked up at the heavens. The stars were wheeling and the moon had climbed high.

'Remember Snakesburg?' he said.

Slessor nodded. 'They were good times,' he replied.

'They sure were. That was one hell of a cow-town. I'd never have got it under control without your help.'

'Those were good days,' Slessor repeated. 'But what's that got to do with anythin'?'

'There's somethin' I have to do, somethin' I might need a little help with. So when I got to thinkin', I figured the best person to have alongside was you.'

'Yeah? And you took the effort to find me?'

19

Barclay laughed. 'It wasn't hard. Ask Ral Craven.'

Slessor spat into the fire. 'I mean to do just that,' he said.

'You might not realize it, but you've got somethin' of a reputation with that gun of yours. I ain't altogether surprised about what you just told me about the Splintered Canyon Bunch. I've heard rumours.'

Barclay's last three words were deliberate but Slessor did not respond to the implied invitation. If there was anything more to his story, he wasn't willing to mention it. They lapsed into silence for a few minutes till Slessor took up the conversation again. 'OK,' he said. 'I guess you'd better tell me just what it is you might be needin' some help with.'

Barclay took a last drag of his cigarette before flicking the butt into the fire.

'It's like this,' he said. 'Some time ago I was workin' for an outfit called the Bar M. It was near a town called Wind

Creek. One weekend some of the boys from the Bar M got into a spot of trouble in town. It wasn't their fault. They got picked on by a bunch of troublemakers workin' for another outfit called the T Bench. Luckily I had some business in town too and I was able to step in and sort things out. Not long after a deputation of citizens turned up at the Bar M offerin' me good money if I would take on the job of tamin' the town. Seems they ain't got no marshal. It's as simple as that. I figured I might need some back up. I got to rememberin' about Snakesburg. The two of us straightened things out there.'

'I can see what the citizens of Wind Creek might get out of this, but what's in it for us?'

'Wind Creek is a real nice town. Or it will be when it's been cleared of the riff-raff that's taken it over. I figure it's the kind of place a man might like to settle down.'

'Are you talkin' about me or about yourself?' Slessor replied.

'I figure we're both in the same situation. I'm gettin' kinda tired of ridin' the range. I figure the time's come to set up on my own. I got some money saved up and together with what I'll make by temporarily takin' on the marshal's job, I reckon I might buy myself a little spread. The railroad has just reached a town called Poverty. That's only about twenty miles away. There wouldn't be any problem shippin' out the beefs.'

'I reckon you don't need me to sort out the place,' Slessor replied.

'We made a good team.'

'Yeah, once.'

'Seems to me we did OK back at the saloon. Anyway, I'm gonna be needin' a reliable foreman if I get this ranch started.'

'Thought you said you wanted help to sort out the town?'

'Yeah, that as well.' Barclay got to his feet and stretched. 'Think about it,' he said. 'Right now I figure I need some shut-eye.' He walked over to the horses and checked that they were settled. Then he returned and spread his bed roll. Slessor was still sitting by the fire. The flames had sunk but the ashes were aglow. Barclay took out his gun and placed it on the ground beside him before closing his eyes.

★   ★   ★

The Green River Trading Post was situated at a ford of the Green River and consisted of a single building of timber construction with a pitched roof made of wood.

'Don't seem to be anythin' unusual about the place,' Barclay remarked. He and Slessor were sitting their horses in the shelter of some trees. They had been observing the scene for some time but had seen nobody coming or going.

'What did you expect?' Slessor said.

'Some sort of activity. How many men do you reckon Ral Craven has at his command?'

'I don't know, but I figure there's a

lot more of 'em than showed up at the Silver Spur.'

'Maybe that no-good coyote who mentioned this place was tellin' you a pack of lies. He'd probably say the first thing that came into his head. The Splintered Canyon Bunch might be far away by now.'

'Well, there's only one way to find out,' Slessor replied. He dug his spurs into the sides of the roan gelding he had acquired at the livery stable and rode out of cover. Barclay followed close behind.

As they approached the trading post, both men were tensed, their eyes searching for any signs of movement. Some hens were scrabbling about in the dust and flew up at their approach. They carried on riding till they finally came to a halt outside the main timber building, where they stepped out of leather and tied their horses to a hitching rail.

Barclay reached for his rifle and Slessor drew his six-gun. They approached the door and pushed at it. It swung open. After the glare of light outside, it took their eyes a few moments to adjust. The store had been ransacked. Shelves had been knocked over and lay in broken pieces; tins and cartons of food lay scattered about; a sack had been ripped open, spilling its contents. Quickly, they passed through a door at the back and checked the rest of the building. It presented the same scene of destruction.

'Looks like we got here too late,' Barclay said.

'There ain't no sign of Walt Brennan and his wife. I don't know them personally, but they're the folks who run the place.'

They moved swiftly outside. Behind the store the river ran in a wide curve and they made their way towards it. As they approached its shallow banks they could see two figures, one of them partly submerged in the water. They ran forward but they knew even before they had knelt down to check that the people were dead. They had both been shot in the back.

'Recognize them?' Barclay said.

'Yeah. It's Walt and his wife.'

'Looks like they were tryin' to get away.'

Slessor got to his feet and sheathed his gun. His face was grim. 'It was cold-blooded murder,' he said, 'but Craven ain't gonna get away with it. Even if he don't come lookin' for me, I'm gonna be lookin' for him.'

Barclay began to look around for sign and it didn't take much effort to find it. A clear trail led down to the river. 'They musta crossed over by the ford. It shouldn't be too hard to follow them.'

Slessor regarded him through hooded eyes. 'I thought you said you had business in Wind Creek?' he said.

'Yeah. I figure we both have. But that can wait. We got other business to settle first. If I didn't already have sufficient reason to want to deal with the Splintered Canyon Bunch, I have now.'

A faint smirk that was actually more of a grimace twitched the corners of

Slessor's mouth. 'I've reached a decision, too,' he said. 'First Craven and his boys; then Wind Creek. Looks like we're ridin' again.'

Barclay nodded. After a moment he held out his hand and Slessor took it. As they shook hands Barclay looked closely at his friend. 'You know,' he said, 'that old woman was right.'

Slessor gave him a puzzled look. 'What old woman?' he said.

'The old woman back at the flophouse.' Slessor's expression was still bemused. 'Never mind. I knocked on her door. She told me you were upstairs. She said it was your right ear that had a part missing. I said it was the left. She was right all along.'

'Glad to know I can still make an impression,' Slessor said.

2

The town of Poverty lay blistering in the sun. The blinds were drawn at the windows of the local newspaper, the *Clarion*, but it didn't make much difference. The offices were hot and stuffy and in the room where the presses stood the air was like a blast from a furnace. The proprietor, Bob Foulsham, stood in the doorway, mopping his brow, when a figure he didn't recognize approached him. He expected the stranger to pass by but to his surprise the man stepped up to the boardwalk and handed him a sheet of paper that he had been carrying in his hand.

'I want that printed in the next edition,' he said. Foulsham's practised eye assessed the stranger. He didn't like the cut of him. He looked mean and shifty and he wore his guns low.

Turning his attention to the piece of paper, he began to read.

NOTICE TO ALL CATTLE MEN. Ship your cattle at greatly reduced rates. Commodious enclosures now available at Horned Toad Head, fifteen miles out of Poverty. All conveniences for prompt shipment available.

There were some further particulars but Foulsham didn't bother reading the small print. He looked up at the stranger over his spectacles. 'So those new cattle pens are ready?' he said.

'Sure are,' the man answered.

'Hadn't you better put in the name of the company you refer to in the advertisement?' Foulsham said.

The man shrugged. 'Just make sure it goes in the next edition,' he said. Without further ado, he turned on his heel and began to walk down the street in the direction of the Yellow Dog saloon. Foulsham watched him for a few moments and then went inside. A young man in shirtsleeves was sitting at a desk. Foulsham walked up to him.

'Mulhall,' he said, 'things have been a bit slack around here recently but I figure you're the man to hunt down a story.'

The youngster got to his feet and stood expectantly. He was unusually tall and dwarfed the old editor. 'Sure am,' he said.

'Well, try this on. I want you to head out to Horned Toad Head and see what's happenin' with regard to those cattle pens you wrote about recently. And let me see what you've got before you go writin' anythin' up.'

Mulhall nodded. 'I'm right on it,' he said.

★   ★   ★

Ral Craven was in a particularly bad mood. His men had ignored his orders to bring Slessor back alive, and in so doing they had succeeded in getting themselves killed. Not that that mattered very much, but it was still a blow to his pride. Only one man had not been involved in the fracas at the Silver Spur saloon. At least he had been able to make his way back and report that Slessor had apparently left town — although he couldn't be absolutely certain of it. He had seen a man he thought was Slessor ride out in the company of another man. That in itself was bad news. If Slessor had teamed up with someone else, it could make dealing with him just that little bit more difficult.

The gunnie's report seemed to add up; otherwise Craven would have wasted no time in riding on Ghost Hill and dealing with the situation himself. The only positive thing was that his gang had been able to stock up with fresh supplies from the trading post. It had been fun gunning down the owner and his wife. Now that he thought about it, it might have added to the enjoyment to have burned the place. He was getting too soft. The boys needed excitement to keep them happy. Never mind. They would have plenty of opportunities ahead of them. Right now, though, he needed to think about Slessor.

'Prairie Dog,' he said, addressing the man beside him. They were sitting in the mouth of a cave with a good view over a wide stretch of country. Inside, the rest of the gang were gathered around a blazing fire, which sent flickering shadows running over the walls and roof.

'Yeah, boss?' the man replied. He was small with pinched, unshaven features, but his rodent-like appearance wasn't the main reason he had acquired the sobriquet of Prairie Dog. That was more because of his high-pitched squeaky voice; like a prairie dog, he could be relied on to be alert to danger.

'Assumin' Jud is right, and that man he saw ridin' out of Ghost Hill is Slessor, what do you think he would do?'

'The obvious thing is that he would keep ridin' and try to put as much ground between himself and us as he could.'

'The obvious thing?'

'He's done it before. But this time I figure different.'

'Why?'

'Because this time, thanks to Felipe's incompetence, he's been forced into a fight and he's come out on top. There's also this other *hombre* to take into account.'

'So what's your conclusion?'

'That they'll decide to come lookin' for us.'

'Yeah, that's the way I figure it too.'

'I'd like to know who this other man is.'

'So would I, but it don't really signify. There are still only two of 'em.'

'We know Slessor. The way this other fella seems to have handled himself, he ain't no greenhorn either. Maybe they'll split.'

'Maybe. Who knows? I got a feelin' that they'll stick together. In which case, it would make sense to sit tight until they show up. Only I got other irons in the fire.'

'Oh yeah?'

'I want to get on back to Poverty and the T Bench.'

Prairie Dog chuckled. 'There might not be much left of the town by the time we get there if the boys carry on the way they've been doin'.'

Craven grinned. 'It's good for the boys to let off some steam, but you may have noticed that the place is now a rail-head. That means easy pickin's once the cattle shipment business takes off.'

'That why you built those cattle pens?'

'You sure catch on quick. I put a little item in the local rag. Things should be pickin' up right now.'

'So we push on and deal with Slessor later?'

'Yeah. All in good time. I've invested a lot of the money we got from those stagecoach robberies in the cattle trade. I figure to capture the market in shippin' cattle from Poverty to the markets back east. That's my priority right now, and with that amount of money involved, I don't trust anybody.' He glanced down at the rodent-like face of his henchman. 'Always exceptin' you, of course.'

Prairie Dog grinned. 'We could still deal with Slessor before we head for Poverty,' he said.

'We could but there's no hurry. That's where I've been goin' wrong. I've been tryin' to push things. It was a mistake comin' all the way here. No, I figure I'll just wait till that apple falls right in my lap. We'll let Slessor do the runnin' and make him think he's in the drivin' seat. Make it clear to the boys, though, that when we finally come to deal with Slessor, I want him alive. I don't care a hoot about this other fella. Maybe he'll drop out and be gone before Slessor ever catches up with us. But I want Slessor to pay the hard way for betrayin' the Splintered Canyon Bunch. He's gonna die, but it'll be real slow.'

★　★　★

Barclay and Slessor spent a considerable amount of time observing the cavern and its surroundings but though it was obvious from the trail they had been following that Craven and his gang had been there, they could detect no sign of movement.

'What do you reckon?' Barclay said.

'I figure they've moved on.'

'We'll be taking a risk gettin' up closer.'

'There's a fair amount of cover. But I'm pretty sure they've gone.'

'OK. We'll leave the horses here and go the rest of the way on foot.'

They hobbled the horses and crept forward, taking a roundabout route so as to avoid presenting an easy target for anyone who might still be there, coming at the cavern from the side. Flattening themselves against the rock walls, they listened closely for any sounds from within. The cavern seemed to exude a hollow breath but they could detect nothing else. Finally, at a signal from Barclay, they sprang forward, their six-guns at the ready. As their eyes adjusted to the gloom, they could see that the place was deserted. The ashes from the fire and the detritus of the outlaws' occupation told their story. The stumps of a few stogies lay around and an empty bottle of whiskey lay where it had been thrown nearby. After a quick examination they moved back out of the cave and followed a path leading to a stretch of grass, which gave obvious indications of having been where the gang had left their horses. A clear trail showed the direction the outlaws had gone.

'They should be easy to follow,' Slessor said. Barclay nodded and then stood for a moment lost in thought. 'What's up?' Slessor added.

'I'm just thinkin'. That cavern would have been a good place to set up an ambush. I wonder why Craven didn't do it.'

Slessor shrugged. 'I guess we'll find out soon enough.'

Passing by the mouth of the cave

once more, they made their way back to where they had left the horses.

★   ★   ★

Night had fallen. From his vantage point in the foothills, Washington Mulhall could see the lights of Poverty twinkling in the darkness about five miles away. In the opposite direction, the vague dark mass of Horned Toad Head loomed against the sky. There were a few flickering points of light in that direction, too, indicating that some activity was taking place even at so late an hour. He could have ridden out to see the new cattle pens at any time during the day, but his reporter's instincts told him that something might be gained by paying a visit surreptitiously by night. He had already done some checking on the man who had placed the advertisement. He had booked in at the hotel and the clerk had told Mulhall that he had been accompanied by a couple of menacing-looking individuals who had subsequently left. From the clerk's description, they seemed to fit the description of some of the no-goods who had been causing trouble in town. What did that say about the cattle pen situation?

While he sat watching, the fire spluttered as sap from the branches he had thrown on it caught the flames. For a few moments the shadows receded and the circle of flickering light extended to the surrounding trees. A cool wind blew from the hills and from somewhere in the distance there came the lonesome call of a hoot owl. Suddenly, he felt tense. He listened closely for any tell tale sounds but, except for the repeated call of the owl, the night was quiet. He glanced towards where his horse was tethered and saw the outline of its shape against the backdrop of the bushes. It did not seem perturbed but still, something warned him of danger. Just at that moment a figure stepped from the surrounding bushes into the firelight.

'Don't try anythin',' the man said. He was carrying a rifle and Mulhall wasn't about to argue with him.

'Mighty late to be paying a social call,' he said.

'This ain't no social call.'

'How about some coffee?' Mulhall said. 'I just made a pot.'

'Pour me a cup,' the man replied.

Mulhall got to his knees and poured the man some coffee. Straightening up, he held the mug out to him. The man stepped forward, leaning slightly, and as he did so Mulhall dashed the coffee into his face. He staggered back, involuntarily raising his arms to defend himself, and in the same moment, Mulhall flung himself forward and grabbed him by the knees. Over they rolled, narrowly missing the fire. The man was at a disadvantage and Mulhall was able to come out on top and straddle him. With both hands he pressed down on the rifle, forcing it towards the stranger's throat. The man seemed to gain an access of strength and began to resist Mulhall's pressure. There was an explosion and a bullet went screeching among some nearby rocks. The struggle for the rifle continued but Mulhall had again assumed control, pressing the rifle down once more. The man began to choke; his eyes bulged and his mouth twisted in a paroxysm of pain and desperation. He kicked his legs and Mulhall was almost unseated before managing to regain his dominant position. The stranger's face reddened and his body began to grow limp as his struggles grew weaker. His hold on the rifle suddenly slackened and Mulhall tore it from his hands. Jumping up, Mulhall pointed the barrel of the rifle at the man's chest.

'I ought to kill you,' he said, breathing heavily and quivering with the aftermath of the struggle. 'Give me one reason why I shouldn't kill you.' The man lay inert, gasping for breath. 'Go on,' Mulhall hissed. 'Say something.'

For a moment more he stood over his attacker before moving towards the fire where, exhausted, he slumped to the ground. He continued watching the man, the rifle across his knees. Presently the man's laboured breathing grew quieter and then he struggled to his feet.

'Over here! Sit down!' Mulhall ordered.

The man staggered and then collapsed beside the fire. The firelight was sufficient to reveal the dark purple welt across his throat where the rifle had been jammed against it.

'I want some answers,' Mulhall said. The man coughed and put his hand to his throat. Mulhall levered the rifle. 'Start talkin',' he said.

'My throat hurts,' the man replied. 'You've damaged it.'

'That's nothin' to what you were plannin' on doin' to me.'

'I wasn't meanin' no harm,' the man said. 'I just come to warn you.'

'Funny way of doin' it,' Mulhall replied. The man looked again at the coffeepot.

'Mind if I have some this time?' he asked.

Mulhall laughed. 'I thought you said your throat was sore. Help yourself, but remember, I got you covered.'

The stranger picked up the tin cup, which lay where Mulhall had thrown it and poured himself some coffee. Tilting his head back gingerly, he winced as he swallowed. When he had managed a few mouthfuls he looked up at Mulhall. 'The name's Pym,' he said. 'John Pym.'

'Mulhall, Washington Mulhall.' There was silence for a while except for the snicker of a horse. Mulhall couldn't be sure whether it was his own horse or the stranger's.

'Smoke?' Mulhall asked. Without waiting for a reply he reached into his pocket and threw the pouch of tobacco to Pym, who caught it and rolled a cigarette. He tossed it back to Mulhall and they both lit up.

'Funny place to be this time of night,' Pym said.

'I ain't breakin' any law,' Mulhall replied.

'Maybe not, but do you realize you're on private property? This is T Bench land.'

'Didn't see any signs,' Mulhall replied.

'Don't need no signs. Everybody round here knows to keep off. If they don't they soon learn. I guess you must be new round here.'

'I've been around awhile. This is the first I've heard anythin' about stayin' clear of the T Bench. Anyway, what's it to you?'

'I ride for the T Bench.'

'And that involves scarin' folk off? Don't matter what their business, they got to be made aware of the T Bench brand?'

Pym shrugged his shoulders, grimacing again as he inhaled deeply. 'Miss Peyote likes to keep a tight outfit. That's the way the T Bench got to be the biggest ranch around these parts. She don't take to newcomers.'

'Miss Peyote?' Mulhall said. 'She owns the T Bench?'

'Sure does. And don't go gettin' any ideas. She runs the place better than any man. Some people have thought otherwise now and again, but they didn't think that way for long.'

'Sounds like quite a lady, although I ain't exactly sure about her methods.'

'Whatever you think, you'd do best to take the warnin' and keep well away.'

'Why are you tellin' me all this?'

'Let's just say I don't like the idea of anyone stirrin' up trouble for Miss Peyote.'

'You've got me intrigued,' Mulhall said. 'Sure, I've heard of the T Bench, but before you appeared out of those bushes it didn't signify anythin'. But now you got me thinkin'. Maybe I'll take a ride out and pay Miss Peyote a visit. Just neighbourly, like.'

'I wouldn't advise it.' Pym got to his feet. 'What about the rifle?' he said. Mulhall split the rifle and ejected the bullets. 'Here, take it,' he replied. Pym accepted the proffered weapon and nodded his head.

'Thanks,' he said. 'Appreciate it. Don't worry; you won't get any more trouble from me.' He seemed to hesitate. 'Don't ignore what I said, though. Really, it wouldn't be wise to do anythin' that might put you on the wrong side with the T Bench. Miss Peyote has some mean people workin' for her. I don't say I always agree with everythin' she does, but the T Bench is not an outfit to be meddled with. Miss Peyote has a lot of interests.'

'Includin' a stake in those new cattle pens by Horned Toad Head?'

Pym looked at him closely. 'You ask too many questions,' he said.

'It's my job.'

Pym opened his mouth as if about to say something else, but whatever it was he thought better of it. Instead, he turned and walked away, disappearing out of the range of the dwindling firelight. Mulhall lay back with his hands behind his head gazing up at the stars. After a time he heard the muffled sound of a horse's hoofs.

Well, he mused, *I guess I've been warned. But one thing's for sure. Old Foulsham's instincts weren't wrong about those new cattle pens. He can sure smell a story.* He felt a sudden upsurge of confidence not untouched with gratitude. If Foulsham had enough faith in him to trust him with looking into the matter, it really meant something.

★　★　★

Barclay and Slessor were alert for a possible ambush but as they followed the sign left by Craven and his gang, it was pretty obvious that they were pushing ahead to reach their destination.

'Kinda strange that they seem to be headin' in the same direction as us,' Slessor said.

'Yeah. Guess it's a small world.'

It seemed that the outlaws might be aiming for Wind Creek itself but as they got closer to the township their sign veered off.

'What do you think?' Slessor said. 'Do we carry on followin' 'em or carry on now to Wind Creek?'

'When we started on this affair, you said first Craven and then Wind Creek. I don't figure that anythin's changed.'

They sat their horses and looked about them. The sun was hot and the horses' heads were hanging.

'Where do you reckon they're makin' for?' Slessor asked.

Barclay shrugged. 'The way they've gone leads in the direction of Poverty.'

'What? The other town you were tellin' me about? The new rail-head?'

'That's the place,' Barclay replied. 'Like I said, it's one of the reasons I figure this country would be a good one to start up ranchin' in. The railroad's right there.'

'How far we still got to go?' Slessor asked.

'To Wind Creek? I don't know. About twenty miles.'

Slessor unfastened his bandanna and wiped his brow. 'If Craven is pushin' on, he must have a good reason for it. He must know we're on his tail but it don't seem to bother him. He could be drawin' us on into a trap.'

'What are you drivin' at?'

'I'm just thinkin'. If they're headin' for Poverty, it might be an idea if we didn't make things too easy for 'em by ridin' into town together.'

Barclay thought about it. 'Yeah, I can see some point to what you say,' he replied. 'We don't want to make ourselves an easy target. And I tell you somethin' else that's just occurred to me. Wind Creek ain't too far from Poverty. It used to be a nice town; now it needs cleanin' out. So where did the trouble come from? It seems a bit of a coincidence that Craven and his gang are operatin' not many miles away.'

'You think it could be the Splintered Canyon Bunch involved?'

'Well, it makes sense.'

They continued to sit in silence,

considering what they had said to each other. Finally Barclay spoke. 'Those varmints don't know me. How about if I carry on to Poverty and see what I can find? You go on to Wind Creek, get a feel for the place. Book in at the Long Rail Hotel. I'll join you there in a couple of days. We should have a clearer idea about how to go about things then.'

Slessor thought about it for a few moments before replying. 'Sounds OK to me,' he said. They touched their spurs to their horses' flanks and rode on.

3

Next morning Barclay rode into the town of Poverty. It was bigger than he had expected, with a number of hotels, boarding houses, general stores and saloons with high false facades. After boarding his horse at the livery stables, he made his way to the hotel and booked a room. Breakfast was being served and although he had eaten something before leaving Slessor, he made his way to the dining room. After all, he and Slessor had been on the trail for some time and a proper meal served in pleasant surroundings was not without its appeal.

There were few other people in the room as he took his place near a window, which looked out onto the street. The town was becoming busy. Ladies passed on their way to do their shopping, stepping lightly along the boardwalks or trailing their skirts in the dust of the street. A couple of riders passed on horseback and a buggy emerged from an intersection. A little girl came by with a cat in her arms.

After he had finished eating he sat for a little while longer watching the street. He had no definite plan in view except to look around and make some general inquiries. Finally, he rose to his feet and made his way outside. The marshal's office seemed a good place to start and he began to walk in that direction. Ahead of him the girl with the cat emerged from the general store accompanied by a lady who Barclay supposed must be her mother. The lady was carrying a large basket and another parcel was tucked under her arm. The girl put the cat down and it rubbed itself against her legs. Outside a saloon Barclay checked some of the horses fastened to the hitch rail: they carried a T Bench brand burned on their hindquarters.

He had almost passed by when the

batwings flew open and two men emerged on the sidewalk. Unhitching their horses they climbed into leather and began to trot down the street. As they rode past the girl and her mother the cat darted towards them. Suddenly one of the riders wheeled his horse round and deliberately trampled the cat under its hoofs. The woman and the girl both screamed and then the girl ran out into the road. The riders took no notice but rode off in a cloud of dust.

Barclay began to run as fast as he could in pursuit of the riders. One of them slowed and, looking back, fired a couple of shots. It was a token effort, however, as they were more or less out of range. The man shouted something and then spurred his horse on again in pursuit of his partner. Barclay had drawn his gun but quickly replaced it in its holster. He turned back to where the girl kneeled, sobbing, the dead cat in her arms. A little crowd had gathered. People were making comments.

'It's a darned shame.'

'There was no need to trample on the poor animal.'

'Poor kid.'

The woman seemed at a loss what to do. She was distraught herself and her basket and parcel had fallen to the ground. Barclay stooped down and picked them up. He kneeled down beside the girl and put his arm around her. 'Come on. There's nothing to be done.'

'My cat,' the girl was sobbing. 'Please let him be all right.'

Barclay let her sob a few moments longer and then gently raised her to her feet. He bent down and took the cat in his arms. It was bleeding from the nose and mouth and there was blood all down its chest.

'Let's take him away and give him a good burial,' he said. He turned to the lady. 'I'm real sorry this happened, ma'am. Can I escort you and the little girl somewhere?'

The woman nodded. She seemed disoriented and confused. 'We live in

Wheeler Street,' she said. 'It isn't far.'

The three of them began to move away, the crowd parting to let them pass. Comments were still being made but otherwise no one else seemed to want to get involved. They continued down the street till they reached a turning. They were in a more residential area with frame buildings and an occasional cottonwood tree. Towards the end of the street they turned again. They were approaching the edge of town when the woman stopped outside a small house with a dilapidated fence. 'We live here,' she said.

Passing through a loose wicker gate they went along a path and up some steps and into the building, which appeared to be unlocked. Barclay glanced quickly about. The place was small and potentially quite cosy. Some attempt had been made to make it look nice but it betrayed obvious signs of neglect. The curtains at the windows were frayed and some flowers in pots looked skinny and bedraggled. There was a sofa that had seen better days and a few chairs around a square deal table. In a corner was a dresser with dishes and pots and pans. The woman went through a door and re-appeared with a blanket.

'Here, she said, placing the blanket on the sofa. 'Put him down on this.'

The girl had stopped sobbing but tears still flowed down her cheeks. When Barclay laid the cat on the blanket she sat beside it, stroking its fur and looking at it as if she expected it to still be alive. Barclay stood up, feeling suddenly awkward.

'I guess I'd best be goin' now,' he said. 'Will you be all right?'

The lady nodded her head. Barclay turned and was about to go when she said: 'Won't you stay? I'll put some coffee on.' Barclay hesitated. 'It'll only take a moment,' she added.

'If you're sure it's no bother,' Barclay said.

She went through the door into the kitchen and Barclay seated himself on one of the chairs. The girl was still stroking the cat's lifeless body but was not crying any more. Barclay was just thinking that it might be a good idea to bury it when the woman appeared in the doorway with the coffee. He decided it wouldn't hurt to let the girl have a few final moments to say her last goodbyes. The woman put the tray down on the table and poured two cups of coffee into china teacups.

'I want to thank you for all your help,' she said. 'I really didn't know what to do.'

'It's nothin',' Barclay replied. 'I just feel sorry for your daughter. It's not something she should have experienced.'

The woman gave an involuntary shudder. 'It was horrible,' she said. 'Who could do such a thing?'

'Did you recognize either of those men?' Barclay asked. She shook her head. 'Their horses carried the T Bench brand,' Barclay said.

'That wouldn't surprise me,' she

answered. 'The T Bench is just about the biggest ranch around these parts. Some of their cowhands have gotten too big for their boots.'

Barclay was thinking that from what he had seen of the men, they didn't look like regular cowhands. Certainly their behaviour had been more in line with something he would have expected from Craven's gunslicks. He finished his coffee, thinking for a moment about what to say next, when the girl suddenly spoke up.

'Mister,' she said, 'are you going to get those men for killing my cat?'

'Amy, don't be silly,' the woman replied. 'That's not the way to do things, as you well know. This gentleman was kind enough to help us out. Just you be thankful for what he's done.'

'It's OK,' Barclay said. He turned to the girl. 'What was the cat called?'

'Caesar,' she replied.

'Well, what do you say? Is it time we gave Caesar a decent send-off?'

The girl nodded.

'OK if we bury him in the garden?' Barclay said to the woman.

'Yes, of course, but really, you don't have to bother.'

'Fetch a spade, if you've got one,' Barclay replied. He turned to the girl again. 'Amy, would you like to carry Caesar out?'

They went outside. It was around midday and the garden was drenched with sunlight. There was a chinaberry bush in a corner and Barclay quickly dug a hole in its shade. When he had finished the girl laid the cat in it. She had become quiet and serious, affected by the unexpected solemnity of the occasion.

'Goodbye, Caesar. Rest in peace,' Barclay said.

When they had returned inside the house he sat beside her. 'Later you could put something up to mark the spot,' he said. 'He'll always be there underneath.' As he was about to go he turned to the woman one more time.

'The name's Barclay, Jet Barclay.'

'I'm Jean,' she said, 'Jean Sandoz. My husband was part Mexican.'

'Was?' Barclay replied, despite himself.

'He died. I'm a widow.' She hesitated for a moment. 'You must come and visit us again,' she said. 'I can see that Amy has taken to you already.'

'I'd like that,' Barclay replied. 'She's a brave girl. So sorry about the cat.'

He walked through the door and down the path, closing the wicket gate behind him. When he reached the turning, he looked back to see Jean Sandoz standing by the gate. He waved to her as he turned the corner.

★ ★ ★

The day following his night-time encounter with Pym, Mulhall rode out towards the T Bench. He had intended on taking a look at the new cattle pens beneath Horned Toad Head, but the conversation with Pym had turned his thoughts in a new direction. Before setting off, he had made some inquiries at the offices of Aloysius Crump, the local attorney-at-law. That individual had been less than forthcoming, but Mulhall had managed to find out one interesting thing. The land around Horned Toad Head had belonged to the T Bench until very recently, when it had been sold by Miss Peyote to an organization by name of the Craven Land and Cattle Association. Shortly after that the cattle pens had been erected. There was nothing unusual about all that, except that the land had been sold at way below its market value. Mulhall pondered the matter as he rode towards the T Bench, following a trail which led southwest towards a spur of the hills. After an hour's easy canter he arrived at a juncture with another trail. He turned up it and a short distance further along arrived at a sign which read:

T Bench. Keep Out.

'Short and direct,' he said to himself.

61

Lying about the range on either side were piles of wooden poles at various distances. 'Looks like Miss Peyote is thinking of fencing off the place,' he mused. 'Sure don't seem too neighbourly.'

Ignoring the sign he spurred his horse forward. Now that he had apparently entered T Bench territory he rode even more slowly, taking care to observe his surroundings. A few buzzards circled in the air and clouds of flies hung about his face, adding their incessant droning to the drumming sound of the horse's hoofs. Otherwise the range seemed to be shrouded in an oppressive blanket of silence. There was evidence of cattle but so far he had not seen any grazing. He reached forward and touched the butt of his rifle in its scabbard. As he did so he saw a flicker of light from the direction of some rocks over to his right. Instantly he drove his spurs into the horse's flanks, urging it forward. He felt something whistle close by and instantly the reverberation of a rifle shot rang through the air. He kept on riding as a second shot exploded but he was now getting well out of range. Looking behind him for any signs of pursuit, he slowed the horse down to a trot. There was nothing to be seen.

Mulhall was puzzled. Maybe the shots had been meant to kill him but he doubted it. He had ridden pretty close to those rocks. Anyone concealed there would have had a clear view of him. It was too much to expect that whoever fired the shots would have missed him or his horse. No, he concluded, they were meant as a warning, a message that he wasn't welcome. He thought again about Pym. One way or another, the T Bench was going out of its way to be downright threatening. He would have to take extra care. Maybe two warnings was pushing his luck. As if to confirm his conclusion, he hadn't ridden much further when a bunch of horsemen appeared over the crest of a ridge to his right, bearing down on him fast. Perceiving no way he could avoid them, he drew to a halt.

There were five riders in all. He strained his eyes, trying to see if Pym was amongst them, but he didn't recognize anybody. They pulled up and one of them, a tall thin man with a dark moustache and a livid scar over his right eyebrow, came alongside.

'In case you didn't notice the sign, this here is private property,' he snarled. 'I'd be justified in killin' you right now.'

Mulhall eyed him closely. 'I'm beginnin' to get the impression folks just ain't welcome around here,' he replied.

'I'll say it just one time,' the man said. 'Turn right round and git the hell off T Bench property.'

Mulhall quickly weighed up the situation. There didn't seem to be much to be gained by arguing with them. They all looked like real mean hardcases. He had learned plenty already. The time wasn't ripe to force a confrontation.

'Don't want to cause no problems,'

he replied. 'It was sure nice meetin' you boys.' As he turned his horse and began to move away, the man's voice rang out behind him.

'Come this way again, and you're a dead man!'

Mulhall continued to ride, conscious of the men's eyes on his back, till he reached the boundary post. There was something ominous about those poles scattered about waiting to be erected, to shut off the T Bench even further from the rest of the world. Riding along the boundary line he noticed something else which he had not seen before: telegraph wire. Its use would make the fencing in of the range a much more practicable proposition but something in his make-up revolted against it. Touching his spurs to the horse's flanks, he rode away across the free grass.

★   ★   ★

After leaving Jean Sandoz, Barclay spent a lot of time thinking about her and the girl, and it was not till the following morning that he made his way to the marshal's office. When he got there, though, it was to find the door locked. He rattled it a few times before turning away and making his way to the livery stables. The place also served as a forge and the ostler, in his role as blacksmith, was hammering out a long strip of metal as he entered. For a few moments the man continued at his task before plunging the hot metal into a bucket of water. There was a sizzling sound and steam rose into the air. Putting down his hammer and wiping his hand across his brow, the ostler acknowledged Barclay's presence.

'Maybe I caught you at a bad moment,' Barclay said.

The man shook his head. 'Nope. Just about to take a break anyway. Care to join me?'

'Sure, that'd be right neighbourly.'

The man poured out two mugs of coffee. 'Name's Crawford,' he said. 'Joe Crawford.'

'Jet Barclay.'

They sat together on a couple of broken-down chairs that stood just within the doorway. From that vantage point Crawford had a good view up and down the main street.

'I heard about what happened with the cat,' he said.

'Yeah. It was a real shame. The little girl was heartbroken.'

'Something ought to be done about some of those T Bench boys. I ain't sayin' they're all bad but some of them just don't seem to know how to behave.'

'So this sort of thing's happened before?'

The blacksmith nodded. 'Usually at a weekend if a bunch of them come to town to blow off steam. I understand a man wantin' to let his hair down a little but too often it gets out of hand. The way things are headin', this town's goin' to end up no better than Wind Creek.'

'Wind Creek?'

'Yeah. It ain't far from here. Things

there are real bad. And I gather it's some of the same people involved.' He paused. 'You know the T Bench is run by a woman?' Barclay tried not to show surprise. 'Well, seems like that's the case. She goes by the name of Miss Peyote. That ain't no kind of a name for a woman in my book. I don't know, maybe she don't control her cowhands like she ought.'

They sat in silence for a few moments. Barclay was reflecting on what the blacksmith had just told him. He finished the coffee and stood up. 'Say,' he said, 'you wouldn't know where I might find a cat around here?'

Crawford grinned. 'Sure,' he said. 'Matter of fact I got three out back. You'd be doin' me a favour takin' one of 'em.'

It was Barclay's turn to smile. 'Let's have a look,' he said.

They passed through the forge to the yard, beyond which was a corral containing several horses; among them Barclay recognized his own. One cat was sitting on a rail. There was no sign of the other two.

'Will she do?' Crawford said. The cat looked up unconcernedly. It was a tabby. Barclay picked it up gently and stroked it.

'She'll do fine,' he said to the blacksmith. 'Are you sure you can spare her?'

'My pleasure,' Crawford replied. The cat purred and rubbed its head against Barclay's jacket. 'Looks like she's taken to you,' Crawford said.

'If it's OK with you,' Barclay replied, 'I might as well take her round to the Sandoz girl right now. No sense in delay.'

'That's fine with me.'

'I'll be back for the horse later,' Barclay said. He had intended riding straight out but the T Bench could wait. 'How much do I owe you?' he asked.

'Nothing,' the blacksmith replied. 'Like I said, you'll be doin' me a service takin' her off my hands.'

'That's mighty decent of you,' Barclay said. 'I won't forget to mention you.'

'Tell Jean I'll be over to see her soon.'

They went back through the forge to emerge again in bright sunlight. Almost by habit Barclay's eyes swept the main street, watching and observing the layout of the buildings and alleyways. This time there were no horses that might be bearing the T Bench brand.

'Killeen, Rafe Killeen,' the blacksmith said. 'And Logan Sharpe.' Barclay turned back. 'A couple of no-good coyotes who ride for the T Bench. I ain't sayin' they had anythin' to do with tramplin' the cat, but watch out for them.'

'Obliged,' Barclay said.

He started off to walk the short distance to the Sandoz house, carrying the cat inside his jacket. 'Hope I ain't pushin' this too soon,' Barclay said to himself. 'Maybe I should've given the little girl more time to get over things.' He approached the widow's house. As he opened the wicket gate the front door flew open and Amy came running down the steps.

'Mr Barclay,' she said, and then

shouted over her shoulder, 'Mama, it's Mr Barclay.' Just then she caught sight of the tabby. 'I didn't know you had a cat,' she said.

'I don't have a cat.'

'But what about . . . whose cat is this?'

'She's your cat if you want her.'

The girl looked up. Her eyes were glistening and there was an expression of joy mingled with disbelief on her features.

'She hasn't got a name yet. You can call her whatever you want.'

Amy's mouth was wide open. 'Do you really mean I can keep her?' she said.

Barclay smiled and handed the cat over to her. She took it and held it close to her tear-stained cheek. 'She's your cat now,' he said. 'I figure you two are goin' to be real friends.'

'Thank you, thank you,' the girl repeated. 'Mama, come quickly! Look what Mr Barclay's brought.'

Just then Jean Sandoz appeared in

the doorway. Seeing Barclay standing there, she looked flustered. 'Sorry to keep you waiting,' she said. 'I've not long been back from the stage depot.' Barclay gave her a puzzled look.

'I work down there. It's only part-time but it helps. Won't you come in?'

'Why, thank you,' Barclay replied.

Amy was trying to tell her mother about the new cat as they entered the house. Barclay could see right away that it looked different. The place had been cleaned and tidied up; it already had more of a homely air. There were clean curtains at the windows and fresh flowers in the vases. Barclay suddenly wished that he had brought some flowers himself. Jean went into the kitchen and emerged after a short time with coffee and a plate of little iced cakes. She had composed herself and appeared to have grasped the situation with the cat.

'You can see for yourself,' she said. 'She's so happy. Really, Mr Barclay, you shouldn't have put yourself to the bother.'

'No bother,' Barclay said. 'Anyway, it's really Mr Crawford you should thank. It's just nice to see Amy looking happy again.'

Amy had taken the cat into the garden. The sounds of her laughter wafted in through the open door.

'Can I at least offer you something in payment?' Jean said.

'One of these cakes is payment enough,' Barclay said. 'I haven't tasted such delicious home cooking in a long time.'

'It's nice to have someone to cook for,' Jean replied and then realizing that she might have said something out of turn she added: 'apart from Amy, I mean.'

Barclay ate three of the cakes. When he had finished he stood up to take his departure.

'Make sure you come and see us again,' Jean said. Outside, Amy came running up to him.

'Are you leaving already?'

Barclay bent down and stroked the cat. 'Take care of each other,' he said.

'We sure will,' Amy replied.

Barclay walked down the path and out into the street. This time he didn't look back but kept walking till he reached the livery stables. Crawford stopped what he was doing at Barclay's approach.

'Thanks,' Barclay said. 'You've helped make that little girl happy again.'

'Kids are durable,' the blacksmith replied. 'They pretty soon get over things.'

Barclay glanced at the stalls behind the forge. 'I'm gonna be needin' my horse pretty soon,' he said.

'He's ready when you want him. Are you aimin' on goin' somewhere in particular?'

'Thought I might take a ride over to Wind Creek,' Barclay replied.

The blacksmith snorted. 'You'd better take care,' he said. 'Like I said, that place is all gone to hell.'

Barclay realized he hadn't been giving a lot of thought to Slessor and how he might be getting on in Wind Creek. He looked up at Crawford. 'Thanks again for the warning,' he said. 'I'll be on my guard.'

* * *

Mulhall sat in the dining room of the hotel. There was a good number of people sitting at the tables and others coming in and going out through the door. In the street there was quite a bustle of activity for a small place. It was getting that way since the arrival of the railroad. Men hustled by, riders passed, saddled horses lined the hitch rails. When he had finished his coffee, he got to his feet and, making his way out of the hotel, began to wander down the street. He continued on his way till he came to the railroad tracks. He crossed to the other side and looked up and down the track. Away down the line he could see a locomotive approaching, a plume of smoke blowing back from its cabbage-head smoke-stack. It was not long after noon.

The train drew closer like a serpent unwinding its length. It breathed out smoke and ash and sparks of fire and its voice was the hissing of steam and the clanging of a bell. There were a few people further down the platform waiting for the train to arrive. The clatter of the wheels on the tracks and the chugging of the engine grew louder and louder and then, with a screeching of brakes, the train drew into the station.

Doors clashed and people alighted, most of them making for the section house, which doubled as a dining hall. Among them were two figures, one of whom he immediately recognized as Pym. He was in the company of a lady whose plain blouse and skirt only seemed to emphasize her beauty. Although she was small in stature, there was something imposing about her. Mulhall had only seen her once before in town, but he wasn't likely to forget her. Instinctively he shrank back into the shadows as they walked towards him. He was puzzled about who she might be and the relationship between them, till he suddenly realized in a flash of inspiration that she was Miss Peyote, the owner of the T Bench, and that the relationship was one of infatuation on Pym's part and indifference on hers. Certain pieces of the puzzle he had been trying to construct fell into place. The reason for Pym warning him off the T Bench was clearer. He had done so because he was trying to protect the woman from his prying. That could only mean she had something to conceal. He shrank back into the shadows of the station building as they swept past and then followed them as they continued up the street.

They came to a stop outside the bank; after a brief conversation she went inside and Pym disappeared round a corner. Mulhall waited. It wasn't long till Pym reappeared driving a buckboard. He brought it to a halt outside the bank and after what seemed an unaccountably long time, Miss Peyote re-emerged and was helped up into the seat on which a number of blankets and cushions had been arranged.

Watching closely, Mulhall was surprised to see that she looked older than he had at first thought. Pym climbed back up to the driving seat and with a flick of a whip, urged the horses forwards. Mulhall watched as they travelled up the street. As they passed a junction a couple of riders swung out and joined them, riding a little way in their rear. Mulhall was sure they were T Bench ranch-hands. He wondered what Pym made of them. He had a suspicion that Pym wasn't altogether comfortable about some of the types she seemed to employ.

4

Barclay felt some guilt at taking up Jean Sandoz's invitation to visit her and Amy. He realized that he had barely given thought to Slessor but he could not resist the prospect of seeing her again. In fact, he had gone further and hired a buggy from the blacksmith. When he arrived at the Sandoz house, Jean seemed shy but she was obviously pleased to see him again. Barclay directed her attention to the buggy. 'I hope I'm not bein' presumptuous, but I'm invitin' you and Amy for a ride.' She looked uncertain but only for a moment.

'That would be lovely,' she said.

Amy didn't need any persuading and by the time the three of them were seated inside they were all in high good spirits.

'Mr Barclay, I've thought of a name

for my new cat,' Amy said as she stroked the creature sitting on her knees.

'Yes? What is it?' Barclay replied.

'Tabitha. You see, she's a tabby and I think that Tabitha was an old Roman name.' She suddenly looked sad. 'It kind of follows on from Caesar.'

'Well, that sounds a very good name to me,' Barclay replied. They bowled on; the sun came out from behind a cloud and Amy quickly recovered her spirits.

'You both know this place better than me,' Barclay said. 'Have you any preference about where we should go?'

They decided to drive up towards the hills. The sun was hot but as they began to approach the foothills a pleasant breeze blew down.

'Isn't it lovely,' Jean said. 'I love this place. When my husband was alive we used to ride up into the hills as far as Horned Toad Head.' She showed no embarrassment talking about her husband. On the contrary, it seemed to come naturally to her. The girl showed no sign of being uncomfortable, either.

'We could go up that way,' Barclay said. 'If it's not too far.'

'I'm not sure I could find my way to it now,' Jean answered, 'but it doesn't matter in the least. Let's just leave it to chance.'

She had made a picnic and they halted to eat it in the shade of some trees by a shallow stream which came down from the hills. When they had finished and Amy was clearing the remnants she turned to Barclay.

'You'll be careful, won't you?' she said unexpectedly. 'The last deputy handed in his badge after a run-in with some of the T Bench cowboys. I wouldn't want you to get involved with them.'

'I think I already have,' he said. 'But don't worry yourself none. I've been around a long time. I intend to keep it that way.'

She looked at him for a moment longer before her gaze fell. Barclay was suddenly keen to change the subject. He stood up and helped Jean to her feet. Together they walked down to the stream to drink the sparkling water. Sunlight glinted on the surface of the stream and some small silver fish darted in and out of the shadows. When they had finished drinking Barclay turned to her. Her mouth and chin were wet and her hair had become loosened. Something about her threw him off balance for a moment and finally all he could think to say was that they had better be starting back. Gathering up the last remains of the picnic they climbed into the buggy and Barclay pulled on the reins. The horse set off at a gentle pace.

'I enjoyed today,' Jean said.

'We must do it again,' Barclay replied.

It was late in the afternoon by the time they arrived back. Jean invited Barclay inside but this time he declined. It had been a good day and somehow he didn't want to do anything that might jeopardize it in any way, although he would have been hard put to say what that might be. Waving goodbye, he drove the buggy back to the livery stable.

Crawford was sitting in his chair by the entrance to the forge and got to his feet at Barclay's arrival.

'You had a couple of visitors,' he said.

Barclay jumped down from the buckboard. 'Yeah?' he replied. 'Who?'

'Rafe Killeen and Logan Sharpe.'

Barclay didn't say anything. He returned the buggy to the back of the building and then helped the ostler to bed the horse down for the night. When they were finished they both sat by the door to watch what was happening in the street. It was quiet with few people about.

'Wonder what they wanted,' Crawford remarked.

'Who?' Barclay answered.

'Killeen and Sharpe.'

'I'd have thought that was pretty obvious.' Barclay's thoughts were on other things. He was reflecting on the day's ride into the hills and on how much he had enjoyed himself. The ostler must have read his thoughts because he suddenly remarked: 'A real nice lady — Jean Sandoz, I mean.'

'Sure is,' Barclay replied.

'She's doin' a good job bringin' up that little girl,' Crawford continued. 'It can't have been easy for her since Sandoz died.'

'What happened to him?' Barclay said.

'He was quite a bit older than her. Mexican. He used to run some kind of general store in Texas down near the border. Apparently he was lugging some big sacks into the shop when he just keeled over. The doctor said it was his heart. At least he left Jean pretty well provided for. She carried on runnin' the store for a while but in the end she sold it and moved away. I ain't too sure why she chose to live in Poverty.'

'Seems a nice town,' Barclay said. 'She could have done a lot worse.'

Dusk had fallen when Barclay finally took his leave. It was a short walk to his hotel but he decided to take a longer way round and enjoy the cool of the evening. The streets were deserted now but from the doors of the saloon the tinkling of a piano could be heard. As he came abreast of it the batwings suddenly flew open and a man appeared on the boardwalk.

'Barclay!' he shouted. 'I got some business with you.'

Barclay halted. The man was dressed in a frock-coat, which was thrown aside to give easy access to the guns slung around his waist. From behind him came another man, shorter than the first but with the same mean look. Barclay observed them closely, weighing up angles and deciding which to go for first should it come to a showdown.

'You hear me, Barclay! I said I got business with you and I aim to settle it right here and right now!'

Still Barclay remained silent as the two men stepped off the boards and walked slowly towards him; it was clear that there was no way to avoid a confrontation. He had worked out which man he was going to aim for first. While the man in the frock-coat was talking, the other man's hand had moved closer to the handle of his gun and was hovering nervously in the air just above it. Barclay noticed he had a crosswise draw. It might slow him momentarily but they both looked like accomplished gunslingers, men who made their way by the gun. He had no doubt that it was Killeen and Sharpe who confronted him.

'You made a big mistake interferin' over that damned cat,' the man continued. 'Now you're goin' to die like a dog, like the dirty dog you are. Do you hear me?'

Barclay was watching the man's eyes for any flicker which might indicate that he was about to draw when in his peripheral vision he saw the other man's hand suddenly drop towards his gun. Almost instantly his own Smith &

Wesson was in his hand and spitting lead. The man reeled backwards and in the same moment Barclay dropped to one knee and taking the barest moment to steady himself, fired again. Two guns exploded in the same instant but it was the man in the frock-coat who lurched back, blood pouring from a hole in his chest. Gathering up all his strength he succeeded in steadying himself but as he fired once more Barclay's final bullet smashed into his face. He managed to stay upright for a second or two; then he crashed to the ground like a felled tree and lay motionless in the dirt. Barclay turned to the other man. He was lying flat on his back, twitching spasmodically.

Getting to his feet again, Barclay walked over to where he lay. The man's face wore a look of surprise but the eyes were blank pools of nothingness and with a final shudder he stiffened and died. Barclay looked up and down the street. It was still deserted but the doors of the saloon sprang open, spilling a few of its inmates onto the boardwalk.

'Get Doc Smith!' somebody shouted. Another man came over to where Barclay stood.

'Better get the undertaker,' Barclay said.

More people were running towards the scene and at the back of them Barclay saw the figure of the marshal. He came forward through the gathering crowd.

'OK, folks,' he shouted. 'Show's over. Get back off the street.' Reluctantly people began to move away.

'They gave me no choice,' Barclay said.

The marshal kneeled down and examined the bodies. 'A couple of no-good, gun-totin' polecats,' he said. 'They had it comin' a long time.' The undertaker came up in a wagon and the three of them loaded the bodies on board.

'Better inform Miss Peyote at the T Bench about what's happened,' the marshal said.

Now that the marshal had arrived on the scene, Barclay was tempted for a moment to ask him a few questions concerning Craven and the Splintered Canyon Bunch, but thought better of it. The marshal seemed to be quite well disposed towards him but the time didn't seem appropriate. He could always approach the lawman on a subsequent occasion. However, he had a feeling that would be unnecessary because he already had the answers.

The wagon lumbered off, raising dust, which shimmered in the light of the setting sun. Barclay made his way to the hotel and it was only when he had taken off his shirt that he became aware that he had been slightly wounded. A bullet had burned its way across his left shoulder. It didn't amount to much and he reached into his war-bag for some iodine. Taking out his six-guns he filled the empty chambers with bullets and then, feeling tired after the various events of the day, flung himself down on the bed, laying the gun on the pillow beside him. He didn't light the lamp and night descended, filling the room with shadows. Lying there in the darkness, he tried to get his thoughts into some sort of order.

There was little doubt in his mind that there was a connection between the T Bench and the Splintered Canyon Bunch, and he thought he knew what it was. He had seen little evidence of Craven or his gang. So where were they? He had more than a suspicion that the T Bench held the answer. Apart from what he had been told concerning the ranch, he had personal experience of its employees. People like Killeen and Sharpe were indistinguishable from the type of gun-slinging desperados who made up the Splintered Canyon Bunch. So the obvious conclusion was that there was no difference. The T Bench was where Craven was hiding out. If that was the case, then it raised another question: who was Miss Peyote and what was her role?

What was less clear to him was the

state of his feelings with regard to Jean Sandoz. Meeting with her had been totally unexpected. It was, to say the least, inconvenient to have to leave Poverty just at the present juncture. But he had arranged to meet Slessor in Wind Creek. He felt slightly guilty about his old friend; the way things had gone since his arrival in Poverty had left him little time to think about him. He had got so caught up with Jean Sandoz that he had neglected the reason why they had both ridden so far. Yet it was he who had sought out Slessor. How had he been getting on? After all, it was the trouble in Wind Creek rather than Poverty that they had come to sort out.

Thinking of Slessor made him ponder again over his friend's odd behaviour in Ghost Hill. Had he been quite ingenuous in attributing his strange defeatist behaviour to the difficult times he said he had been going through? Or was there something more involved, something Slessor either hadn't been able or prepared to mention? Slessor had perked up once they had been reunited, but was there a danger he might have relapsed? The time had come to make his way to Wind Creek. After that, it was in the hands of the gods.

*　*　*

Once he had left Poverty behind, Barclay rode on without stopping till he arrived at Wind Creek. Leaving his horse at the livery stable, he made for the barbershop. For half an hour he relaxed among the soapsuds in a tin bath and then lay back in the barber's chair. As he stropped the razor, the barber kept looking out of the window.

'Expectin' someone?' Barclay asked.

The barber shifted his gaze away from the street but didn't reply. Laying the razor down, he mixed up shaving foam in an enamel bowl and began to lather Barclay's face. Barclay felt relaxed. He closed his eyes and barely registered the sound of the door to the barbershop opening and closing. A slight pinprick made him open his eyes.

'Sorry, sir,' the barber said.

The barber had nicked him and he began dabbing at the cut with a towel. Reflected in the mirror were the faces of two hard-looking men. They were both stubbled; apart from that they didn't look as though they were in need of a barber's services. Barclay's eyes met theirs and held them in a steady gaze. The barber had managed to stem the bleeding but it seemed to Barclay that his hand was a trifle unsteady as he finished the job. Barclay stood up. Neither of the men made to move. One of them spat a chew of tobacco and looked up at Barclay from hooded eyes.

'Passin' through?' he asked.

Barclay weighed them up. They were both wearing guns.

'That sorta depends,' he replied. Paying the barber, he walked out into the sunlight. As he looked up and down, the door opened and the two men stepped out behind him. Ignoring them, Barclay began to make his way down the street. As he walked he kept his eyes open for Slessor. It wasn't a big town and there was every chance that he might see him. Thinking of Slessor made him change his course and head for the hotel; it might be worth checking that his name was on the register. He stopped to let a buggy pass by and then climbed up onto the boardwalk. The hotel lobby was shady and he paused for a moment to let his eyes adjust before stepping over to the desk.

'Good afternoon. Wanting to book a room?' the clerk asked.

'Nope. I'm meetin' someone. Just wanted to check that he's here.'

'What was the name?'

Barclay gave it and the clerk looked in the register.

'I'm sorry, but there's no one of that name.'

'Let me take a look,' Barclay replied. As he turned to look in the register, he had a momentary glimpse of a figure standing in the darkened entrance way. He glanced back but the figure had already moved outside. Without thinking any further of the matter, he looked in the book.

'Could your friend have signed under some other name?' the clerk asked.

Barclay shrugged. 'Maybe, but I don't see any reason why he would.'

'Can you describe Mr Slessor?'

Barclay grinned. 'Sure, that's easy. He's got part of an ear missin'.' He gave a few other details. The clerk shook his head.

'I'm sorry,' he said. 'I think I would have remembered someone of that description.'

Barclay stood for a moment, thinking. What had happened to Slessor? There wasn't another hotel. Maybe he had found some other type of accommodation? He thought back to the flop-house where he had found him. There was probably some simple explanation, but it certainly seemed that Slessor had not done as they had

95

arranged. 'Thanks,' he said to the hotel clerk. 'Appreciate your help.'

He turned and walked back through the door into the street. He paused for a moment when he heard a footstep. He looked round to see the two men from the barbershop behind him.

'I hadn't finished talkin',' one of them said.

Before he could say or do anything, Barclay's eye detected a sudden movement and then he was struck by a heavy blow just behind the ear. His head exploded in pain as he staggered forwards. The two men were on him, swinging their fists, and he went down hard. As one of the men aimed a boot at him, he managed to roll aside. Getting back on his feet, he sprang at them, lashing out with his fists. He felt the jolt in his arm as he landed a solid blow to the chin of the man who had done the talking. He went reeling back, banging his head against a stanchion as he did so.

Barclay spun round to face the other

man and as he rushed forwards Barclay ducked and rammed his head into the man's stomach. He emitted a grunting sound and Barclay followed up his advantage with a jabbing blow to the man's nose. It split like a ripe apple and blood poured down his face as he toppled backwards. Barclay stepped forwards but as he did so his arms were pinioned from behind.

He could do nothing to defend himself as another man appeared in front of him and crashed his fist into Barclay's solar plexus. The two men who had first accosted him had got back on their feet. Their faces were etched with hatred and Barclay knew he could expect no mercy as they took their revenge, raining blow after blow on his defenceless body both with their fists and their boots. Waves of pain engulfed him but he knew he had to try and hang on as the punishment continued relentlessly. His head rocked from side to side as blows rained down on it and he was only prevented from sinking to the floor by the arms which restrained him. He made one last feeble effort to free himself and then blackness rushed down on him as the pain finally ceased.

When he came round he was lying on a rumpled blanket. A wind rustled overhead. He lay for a long time, trying to work out where he was and how he had got there. He was too hurt to move but at last he felt he must make an effort to do so. His head pounded as he tried to raise it and his whole body ached, but as he finally dragged himself up to a sitting position he realized that someone had already done something to help him because his head and stomach were both swathed in bandages. Who could it be? As if in answer to his question, he heard footsteps and a figure appeared.

'Thought I heard some movement,' a voice said. 'Here, take a sip of this brandy.'

Barclay did as the man suggested. The liquor burned its way down his throat but he felt slightly better for it.

'Where am I?' he managed to say.

'Nowhere in particular,' the man replied. 'The nearest town is a place called Wind Creek.'

'Wind Creek?' Gritting his teeth against the pain, Barclay sat upright.

'I was ridin' by. You were lucky I spotted you.' The man smiled. 'The name's Mulhall,' he said. 'Washington Mulhall.' Barclay introduced himself and they shook hands.

'What happened to you?' Mulhall said. 'You looked like you'd been trampled on by a herd of buffalo.'

'It feels like it,' Barclay replied. In a few words he told Mulhall what had happened to him in Wind Creek.

'Those varmints must have brought you out here and dumped you,' Mulhall replied. 'Like I said, it was just pure chance I came on you.'

Barclay felt his bandages. 'Thanks for helpin' me,' he said. 'I sure owe you.'

'I had a few things in my saddle-bags, but I figure you need to see a doctor.'

'I'll be OK,' Barclay replied. He glanced up at the sky. It had been early afternoon when he had run into his attackers. 'When did you find me?' he asked.

'This morning,' Mulhall replied.

Barclay tried to do some calculations. 'Then I must have lain here overnight,' he said.

'I reckon so. You were in a bad way. You seem to be makin' a pretty good recovery, though.'

Barclay took another swig of the brandy and handed the bottle back to Mulhall, who did likewise. 'Have you got any idea who did this?' he asked.

Barclay nodded. 'Yeah. I got a pretty good idea.'

'You can maybe count yourself lucky they didn't kill you,' Mulhall said.

Barclay attempted to laugh but the effort brought on a spasm of pain. 'Yeah, I guess I gotta count my blessings,' he replied.

Mulhall got to his feet. 'It'll be gettin' dark soon,' he said. 'Why don't I build

up the fire and get some supper goin'?'
He hesitated for a moment. 'If you could manage to eat, that is.'

Barclay summoned up a grin. 'I figure I could put somethin' away,' he said. 'And I would surely appreciate a mug of coffee.'

By the time he had eaten and drunk a couple of cups of black coffee, Barclay was feeling a lot better. He and Mulhall seemed to have established a kind of rapport. The reporter was young and inexperienced, but from what he had told him, Barclay had formed a decent estimate of his ability to look after himself.

'You didn't let this *hombre* Pym put you off taking a look at the T Bench?' he said.

'I took a ride out there but I didn't get too far. I was stopped by a bunch of gunslicks and I didn't feel like takin' them on.'

'You don't figure Pym is one of 'em?'

'He might be, but he doesn't seem the type.'

101

'What do you know about the owner of the T Bench?'

'Miss Peyote? I've been askin' about her. Seems like she took over not too long ago. A rancher by name of Candler used to own it. I know him. He's a nice fella.'

'He didn't say why he sold up?'

'Sure. There was nothin' suspicious about it. He figured he was just gettin' too old.'

'Did he tell you anythin' about Miss Peyote?'

'He never met her. The sale was done through her representative. It was all legal and in proper order.'

'And now she sells off a part of it cheaply to whoever put up those cattle pens.' Barclay paused to fill his coffee cup. 'You say you were makin' for Horned Toad Head when you came across me? Would you have any objections if I rode along with you?'

'Nope. In fact, I'd be glad of your company.'

'Sorry I kind of upset your plans.

You'd have been there before this if you hadn't stopped to take care of me. I sure appreciate it.'

'It's nothin'.'

Barclay was thoughtful. 'I'd like to know what happened to Slessor,' he mused.

'The man you were meant to meet in Wind Creek? Do you intend on goin' back?'

'I've been thinkin' about that and I got a feelin' that I ain't gonna find him there. In fact, I figure he never even got that far.'

'What do you mean?'

'Well, like I was sayin' to you earlier, he seemed to be actin' a mite strange. Maybe it was a mistake to leave him.'

'You mean when you went on to Poverty?'

'Yes. Lookin' back on it, I think it might have been better if we'd stuck together.'

'So if he didn't go to Wind Creek, where did he go?'

'That's the uncomfortable part. I told

you about Craven and his gang. I got a worried feelin' that maybe they caught up with him.'

'You told me he could take care of himself. In fact, didn't you say he had a bit of a reputation with a gun?'

'That's true, but any man can be dry-gulched.'

'Surely he'd have been on his guard?'

'That's what worries me. When I found him back in Ghost Hill, he sure wasn't being too careful.'

'Of course, you could be gettin' this all wrong,' Mulhall said. 'You're talkin' as though he's the victim in all this. Maybe the opposite is the case. Maybe he found somethin'. Maybe he decided to take on Craven by himself without you. After all, it was him that Craven was after in the first place, not you.'

Barclay looked across at his young companion. 'I think I can see why you're a reporter,' he said. 'You sure seem to have a nose for things. You know, I figure you could be right. I could be lookin' at this from the wrong angle. Maybe Slessor is out there right now dealin' with Craven. Hell, if we're right about the T Bench and Craven is usin' it as his hideaway, then that might be just the place we should be lookin' for Slessor.'

'If he's there,' Mulhall replied, 'I hope he didn't meet with the same kind of welcomin' committee that I did.'

'How far is it to the T Bench?' Barclay said.

'About fifteen miles.'

Barclay thought hard. Dusk was drawing down over the distant hills. 'Horned Toad Head is that way, right?' he snapped.

'Yes. In fact, with field-glasses, you might just be able to see it.'

Barclay thought for a few moments more. 'OK,' he concluded, 'this is what I reckon we should do. It'll soon be dark, dark enough for us to take a look at the T Bench without bein' spotted.'

'If we're lucky,' Mulhall interposed.

'We'll make sure we are,' Barclay replied. 'Once we've done that, we can make for Horned Toad Head. It can't be too far further if it used to be part of the T Bench.'

Mulhall grinned. 'Seems like a good plan to me,' he said. Barclay laughed but the effort brought him up sharp.

'Are you sure you're fit enough to be ridin'?' Mulhall asked. 'Those varmints sure roughed you up some.'

This time Barclay contented himself with a grin. 'I'll be fine,' he said.

'What did you find so amusin' anyway?'

'Oh, just that you seem so willin' to go up against Craven and the Splintered Canyon Bunch, especially after what I've been tellin' you about them.'

Mulhall began to kick out the embers of the fire. 'I'm lookin' forward to meetin' them,' he said. 'My boss, Mr Foulsham, figured there was a story in all this, but it could turn out to be a lot more than that. Jumpin' Jehosaphat, I could be headin' for my first scoop.'

5

Stars appeared like blossom on the tree of night as Barclay and Mulhall rode steadily in the direction of the T Bench. There was little doubt about when they had reached it. All along the boundary line fences had either been erected or were in the process of being erected and already a considerable amount of the open range that Mulhall had seen on his former visit had been enclosed. Posts had been placed at regular intervals and wire bound tight to them. In places several strands of wire had been twisted into a cable and fastened to large rocks buried deep in the ground to give added support.

'Miss Peyote's men have been busy,' Mulhall said.

'Sure seems like they intend closin' this place off,' Barclay replied. 'I wonder if they've got somethin' to hide?'

As they continued to ride, Mulhall was surprised to see cattle on the range, which had previously been bare. He drew Barclay's attention to this and the older man brought them to a halt.

'Let's take a closer look,' he said.

They rode up to a group of cattle and dismounted. Barclay approached the nearest cow and bent down to look closely at its markings. He stood up and addressed Mulhall. 'See for yourself,' he said.

Mulhall did as instructed. 'What am I lookin' for?' he asked.

'Those brands. It's hard to tell in the dark, but it looks to me like they've been interfered with. They're carryin' T Bench markin's, but there's somethin' not right about it.'

'Wouldn't they be difficult to alter?'

'No matter how carefully a brand's designed, it can be altered.'

'You think they've been rustled? I ain't heard of any complaints from the ranchers around these parts.'

Barclay considered the young man's

comment for a moment and then slapped his thigh. 'Of course,' he said. He turned to Mulhall. 'Didn't you say that Miss Peyote had sold the land on which those new pens have been built over by Horned Toad Head?'

'Yeah, that's right. So what?'

'She seems mighty keen now to fence in the rest of her land. Maybe Miss Peyote or whoever's involved in this didn't have to resort to rustlin'. Maybe all they have to do is just sit back and have the cattle delivered right to their door.'

Mulhall considered his words for a moment. 'I think I see what you mean,' he said. 'But that would suggest Miss Peyote is definitely involved with Craven.'

'It's a nice set-up,' Barclay replied. 'Cattle are driven up to the rail-head. Craven takes delivery. One way and another, they end up on the T Bench.'

'He'd have to be careful about how he did it,' Mulhall said, 'but he would only need to take a few at a time.'

'It doesn't sound quite like the way the Splintered Canyon Bunch would operate,' Barclay said. 'But I guess it'd be just one more string to Craven's bow.' He glanced around. 'I think we're certainly on to something. The details can wait till later. But right now I figure we need to get movin'. We must be gettin' close to the ranch house. Let's take a look before carryin' on to Horned Toad Head.'

'What we've found here could make that pretty interesting,' Mulhall replied.

They mounted up and rode on. Mulhall seemed to be insensitive to the dangers of their situation, but Barclay was on the alert. His eyes scanned the dusky landscape and his ears were attuned for the slightest indication of hoofbeats. After a short time they topped a rise and saw the ranch house ahead of them. It showed obvious signs of wealth and affluence. The building itself was long and low with a patio and garden. There were numerous outbuildings and one of them, which Barclay assumed was the bunkhouse, was connected to the main building by a kind of roofed-in passage. Trees had been planted at the back and around the sides of the building to provide shelter and protection and there was a rambling pool of water shaded by drooping willows. There were some corrals at a little distance and off to the right stood a windmill whose revolving vanes were, for the moment, stilled.

'Nice spread,' Mulhall remarked.

Barclay was looking closely at the ranch house. No light showed and the place was shrouded in silence. He drew Mulhall's attention to the absence of any signs of activity.

'There's nothin' unusual in that,' Mulhall replied. 'It is kinda late, after all.'

'If the place is occupied by Craven and his gang, I'd expect some sort of indication of it,' Barclay replied. 'In fact, I'm a little bit surprised we've got this far without bein' challenged.'

'We could take a closer look.'

'That's just what I intend doing, especially as Craven seems to be elsewhere.'

'If Craven and his gang ain't usin' this place as their hideout, then we're back to square one.'

'I didn't say that. I figure they make use of this place, all right. Only I reckon it isn't the only one.'

'Where else would they be?'

'At Horned Toad Head. We'd better be very careful when we get anywhere near there.'

They dismounted and, leaving their horses, swiftly and stealthily made their way to the ranch house. Creeping up to the window, Barclay peered through a gap in the curtain. The room was dark and deserted. He stepped down from the veranda and they crossed the yard past the bunkhouse to the corrals. There was space for plenty of horses but there were only a few occupants. Barclay peered closely at them and then, climbing over the rail, approached the shadowy outline of one which stood in the far corner of the corral. He looked closely at it before returning to Mulhall.

'What is it?' Mulhall asked.

'That chestnut gelding is Slessor's horse.'

'What! Are you sure?'

'Yeah I'm sure.'

'Do you reckon Slessor's here some-place?'

'Seems a fair assumption.'

They paused, glancing about them. Above their heads the constellations circled: Perseus, Cassiopeia, Orion with its sword piercing the eastern horizon. The moon had risen and hung low and yellow. Just at that moment Barclay detected a flicker of light at an upstairs window.

'There's somebody up there,' he said, pointing.

'I can't see anything.'

'Wait a moment.'

They waited patiently and after a few minutes the light re-appeared. This time it was in a window of the main room.

'I reckon it's a candle,' Barclay said. 'I guess the curtains don't quite shut it out.'

Without saying anything further, they both began to move towards the curtained window. They had almost reached it when suddenly the drape was pulled aside and a face appeared, looking out into the night. Instinctively, they both dropped to the ground.

'Do you think we were seen?' Mulhall breathed.

'Nope.' Barclay began to shuffle forwards. The face had disappeared but after a moment it appeared again. Barclay could hardly prevent himself from gasping and giving the game away. He waited a moment, pressed flat to the ground and not moving. The curtain closed and he turned to Mulhall.

'I don't know what's goin' on,' he said. 'But I'm certain that was Slessor at the window.'

Mulhall was about to reply but Barclay signalled for them to move back again. They shuffled backwards and then got to their feet. Doubled over, they reached the shelter of the corral. No sooner had they done so than a door opened and two figures emerged. They moved towards the corral and for an anguished moment Barclay thought they had been spotted. When they were within a matter of yards the two figures turned and began to walk towards the open country. The figures were those of a man and woman and they were walking hand in hand.

'It's Slessor,' Barclay whispered.

'And the woman with him is Miss Peyote. I only recently saw her but I'd swear to it.'

'I don't see who else it could be,' Barclay replied. They waited in silence while the two figures disappeared into the darkness.

'Come on,' Barclay said. 'Let's get out of here. I don't want to take any chances on being discovered.'

With a last glance around them they began to move as swiftly as they could in the direction of the ranch house. As they passed the door Barclay hesitated for a moment.

'Do you think we should take a look?' Mulhall breathed.

Barclay had momentarily considered it but shook his head. 'Slessor could be back any moment. I doubt whether we'd find anything. I think I've seen enough.' They moved swiftly past the ranch house and kept going till they reached their horses.

'What do you think's goin' on?' Mulhall said.

'I don't know. You're the ace reporter. What do you reckon?'

'One thing seems pretty obvious. Slessor and Miss Peyote sure seemed to be more than a mite friendly.'

'Yeah!' Barclay grunted. He didn't like to think about what that might signify. After seeing Slessor and Miss Peyote together, he wanted nothing better than to get back into the saddle and press on to Horned Toad Head. Without further ado they climbed into leather and began to ride.

There was no mistaking their destination. Long before they got close to it, the towering mass of rock in the shape of a toad's head loomed large in front of them, obscuring a slice of sky. The trail took them underneath its huge shadow and down the other side towards the plain beneath. As they rounded a corner of the bluff, they saw the dark shape of shacks and the scattered outline of cattle pens. The wind had been at their backs but as they descended the winding trail a sudden gust brought the smell and sounds of cattle.

'Better not get too close,' Barclay said. 'We don't want to scare those cows with the smell of our horses.'

They came to a halt and slid from leather. Barclay reached into his saddle-bags and produced a pair of field-glasses. Settling down behind a rock, he took a long, close look. A thin plume of smoke arose from a couple of the shacks and in one of the corrals a bunch of horses were gathered.

'Looks like we were right about Craven and his gang,' Barclay said.

'You mean about this place being their hideout?'

'Yeah. And it looks like they're there in occupation right now.'

'What about the T Bench?'

'I figure they must make use of that as well.'

'In that case, what was Slessor doin' there?'

Barclay didn't respond at once but, looking at him in the starlight, Mulhall could see from the set of his jaw that his mood was grim. Barclay handed him the glasses and he took time to take a look at the scene below. Beyond the line of shacks and corrals gleams of starlight glinted on the railroad tracks that stretched across the blackness of the flatlands. He glanced over his shoulder to where the immense shape of Horned Toad Head cast its giant shadow. Barclay was still sunk in silence.

'There's got to be a logical explanation,' Mulhall ventured as he handed back the field-glasses.

'Maybe,' Barclay said. 'But I can't see how Miss Peyote can be anything other than a member of Craven's gang. In which case, where does that leave Slessor?'

'You've known him for a long time. You've ridden with him. You can answer that question better than me.'

'Yeah, but I can only see one answer.'

Suddenly Mulhall had an inspiration. 'Maybe Slessor tracked Craven to the T Bench but when he arrived Craven and his gang had already left for here.'

'Even if that were the case, what was he doin' with Miss Peyote?'

'It might not have been how it looked.'

Barclay looked at him closely. 'Hold on,' he said. 'You've just given me an idea.'

'What? I only said — '

'Listen. It was Slessor who broke up the Splintered Canyon Bunch. He was the one who put Craven behind bars and shot his brother. He told me that

119

much. But he didn't go into any details. He didn't say how he got involved with Craven in the first place. I figured it was just chance, that he was simply actin' in a role as lawman. But what if his involvement went deeper than that? I lost touch with him after we cleaned up Snakesville. I don't know what sort of company he got mixed up with. What if he somehow ended up on the other side of the law? What if his association with the Splintered Canyon Bunch was more intimate than that?'

'You figure he might have been a member of the gang?'

'I don't know. I'm just thinkin' out loud. But if he was, and Miss Peyote was involved, too, then his connection with her might go further and deeper. Describe Miss Peyote to me again.'

'There's not much to describe. As far as I could make out, she's a good-lookin' woman.'

'Didn't you say somethin' about her lookin' older than you expected?'

'Yes. I don't know just what I did

expect, but she certainly looked older than Pym.'

'He's the fella you said warned you off the T Bench?'

'Yeah, that's him. And somehow I got a feelin' he ain't gonna be any too pleased about Miss Peyote bein' friendly with your friend Slessor.'

'If you're right about Miss Peyote, it would fit,' Barclay mused. He paused, seemingly quite agitated. 'If Slessor knew Miss Peyote from the past,' he concluded at last, 'it still doesn't tell us what he was up to renewin' old acquaintances.'

They sat their horses, both of them thinking hard, while the first tints of dawn began to show on the horizon. Suddenly their reverie was disturbed by the boom of a gun. The echo went ringing around the rocks. Barclay looked up and saw a stab of flame. A second shot went singing over their heads while down below a blaze of lights appeared.

'Somebody's seen us!' Barclay

rapped. 'Come on, let's get out of here!'

They dug their spurs into the flanks of their horses but as they galloped down the slope leading to the cattle pens, they realized they were in a fix. Men were pouring out of the shacks below and running to the corrals to mount their horses. If they carried on, they would ride straight into them. On the other hand, if they turned tail and retraced their steps up the trail towards Horned Toad Head, they would be making themselves a target for whoever had opened fire on them. Barclay searched the terrain for an alternative and was rewarded when he detected a narrow trail leading away to their right. He was riding just ahead of Mulhall and he shouted to him to follow. The trail led along the slope of a hill. It soon narrowed and seemed like it was going to peter out but Barclay's horse kept on going. They splashed through a little mountain stream and found themselves among some trees. Mulhall shouted something but Barclay couldn't make it out. The narrow trail dipped down into a draw and it was only as he came up the opposite slope that Barclay saw the riders. There were three of them, sitting their horses with their rifles raised, barring the way ahead. There was nothing Barclay could do but bring his horse to a halt as Mulhall came up behind him.

'That's far enough,' one of the men said. He was small and spoke in a high-pitched voice.

'Why don't we just shoot 'em, Prairie Dog?' one of his companions grunted.

'Shut up!' Prairie Dog replied. He turned to Barclay. 'Throw down your guns,' he piped.

Barclay quickly weighed up the options and decided that, for the moment, discretion was the better part of valour. The rifle barrels of the two men sitting alongside of Prairie Dog were pointing straight at him and Mulhall. If he had been alone, he might have taken a chance, but he had a responsibility to take the younger man into account.

'Do as he says,' he snapped. Reaching forwards, he drew out his rifle and threw it to the ground; Mulhall did likewise.

'And now the gun-belts. Take it real easy. These boys have got itchy trigger fingers.'

When they had undone their gun-belts and thrown them down also, Prairie Dog urged his horse forward till he came close enough to get a clear view of Barclay. 'You made a big mistake, Slessor,' he said.

Barclay was thinking hard. Evidently, Prairie Dog had mistaken him for Slessor; he had been expecting him. He hadn't been in the original gang so he couldn't know what Slessor looked like. The fact that he was wrong also meant that he couldn't know that Slessor was back at the T Bench. Mulhall's surmise was correct. Slessor must have arrived at the T Bench after Craven and at least the majority of his gang had already left.

'What's this all about?' Barclay said

non-committally. 'We were just takin' a ride.'

'Don't try to get clever. Nobody takes a ride at this time of night. Besides, this land is private.' Prairie Dog turned to the other two riders. 'Let's take them in, boys,' he said.

The other two came up alongside and they set off down the trail, Prairie Dog leading the way. After a short distance the trail unexpectedly broadened and they emerged on a shoulder of the mountain. Behind them the hulking shape of Horned Toad Head loomed menacingly. They turned in the opposite direction and soon came in sight once more of the shacks and corrals marking the site of the new cattle pens. As they descended, another group of horsemen appeared, coming up the trail towards them.

'It's OK, boys, we got him!' Prairie Dog called as they drew nearer. The new bunch of horsemen came to a halt as Prairie Dog came up to them.

'Is it Slessor?' the leader of the group remarked.

'Sure. Who else would it be snoopin' about? Craven was right. We only had to sit tight till Slessor fell right into our laps.'

'Craven's gonna be mighty pleased about this. But what are we gonna do with them till he gets back?'

Prairie Dog thought for a few moments. When he spoke there was a knowing gleam in his eye.

'If I know Craven, he ain't gonna be wastin' any time ridin' out here. He's gonna be headed for the T Bench.' The others each gave a coarse laugh. 'It'll make things even better if he finds Slessor waitin' for him comin' as well as Miss Peyote.'

'You figure we should take them back to the T Bench?'

'Sure. What else? And after a day or two with Craven, they'll be pleadin' for mercy.'

Barclay listened closely to what the rodent-like little man was saying. It was clear to him that the only thing that had saved them from being shot on sight was that Prairie Dog had mistaken him for Slessor. For whatever reason, Craven wanted Slessor alive, at least for the time being. Their best chance of survival was to maintain the charade. He would have liked to indicate this to Mulhall but there was no chance of speaking to the young reporter without being detected. Mulhall was no fool, though. He appeared to have grasped the situation. They had been given a reprieve; that was all. Craven was clearly somewhere else. From what the gunslick had said, it seemed they had at most a couple of days till he returned. Where was he? What was he up to? In any event, their reprieve was to be short lived. Once Craven got back, he would know instantly that he, Barclay, wasn't Slessor. Craven wasn't likely to be very pleased about it. After that their time would be very short. For some reason, he suddenly found himself thinking of Jean Sandoz.

Later that same morning, the lady in question was sitting at her desk at the stage line office in Poverty. Now that the railroad had arrived, the stage was under threat of going out of business and although she only worked for part of her time, Jean was more than a little worried about her future. For the moment, however, business remained comparatively brisk and a little group of passengers had already taken their seats aboard the coach. Through the doorway two men appeared carrying a small express box, which they hoisted up and placed behind the driver's seat. The shotgun guard swung himself up and with a crack of the driver's whip, the stagecoach rolled out of the yard. Jean had got up from her seat to watch it; looking back, the guard caught a glimpse of her trim figure before she was lost in a swirl of dust.

An hour passed and the horses strained at the collar. The road was climbing and the sun burned in the heavens. The driver knew how to treat his horses and as they began to lag, he brought them to a halt. He kicked on the brake and leaned over the side of the coach to call out to the passengers.

'We're taking a stop. Get out and take a stretch if you want to.'

The doors were pushed open but even before the passengers had alighted a shot rang out and the guard tumbled from the roof of the stage, hitting the ground with a thud. From out of the bushes four men appeared. They were masked and their guns were drawn. Quickly, they stepped to the coach and began to fire inside. There were screams from within and then a sinister silence. The leader of the men stepped to the driver's side.

'OK, throw down the box!' he ordered.

'You won't get away with this,' the man began but got no further as a couple of bullets ripped into his hapless body.

'He talks too much,' the leader remarked to one of his men. 'You get up there and do it.' The man clambered up to the top of the coach, seized the heavy express box and, setting it on the edge, pushed it over. It fell to the earth and rolled on its side.

'OK, grab it!' the leader said. Another of the men sheathed his gun and, lifting the box to his shoulders, carried it into the surrounding brush. The man on the coach jumped down and joined the others.

'Boy, that was easy!' he exclaimed. 'I gotta hand it to you, Craven. You sure know how to pull a robbery.'

Craven pulled down his bandanna and began to laugh. 'Folks ain't gonna forget the Splintered Canyon Bunch!' he ranted. 'And they're gonna pay for what they did to us.'

'You mean Slessor?'

'Yeah. Slessor and anyone else that gets in our way.' He looked about him at the scene of carnage. 'OK, boys!' he shouted. 'Let's get back to the horses.'

The two gunslicks gave a couple of whoops and one of them pulled out his six-gun and began to fire into the air. Craven laughed again.

'Enjoy yourself, Murphy,' he said. 'We've hardly started yet.'

They moved into the trees; in a few minutes the muffled sound of their horses' hoofs told of their retreat — if there had been anyone left alive to hear it.

* * *

Crawford had just laid aside his hammer to take a breather when he heard the sound of voices though the open door of his forge. He looked outside. An agitated crowd had gathered outside the stage depot. Taking off his apron, he began to stride down the street. When he got there the crowd parted and he entered the building. Jean Sandoz looked up at his approach and he could see that she was upset.

'What happened?' he said.

'The stage has been held up and everybody killed.'

'What? Including the driver and the shotgun guard?'

'All of them. This gentleman here found the stagecoach. The marshal has just left to see for himself.' Crawford turned to the man she indicated.

'I was headin' for town,' the man said. 'I just came right on it.'

'Tell me what you found.' When he had finished Crawford turned to Jean Sandoz. 'I'll take you home,' he said.

'I can't leave just at the moment,' she replied. 'Mr Pearson — he's the proprietor — hasn't got here yet.'

'I know who Mr Pearson is. He can handle things. Right now, I think you need to come with me.'

Jean didn't debate the point any further. She took Crawford's proffered arm and he led her away from the depot. As they walked towards her house, she seemed to recover something of her poise.

'It's terrible,' she murmured. 'All

these things happening in Poverty. It never used to be like this.'

They turned the corner into her street. Crawford wanted to take her mind away from dwelling on what had happened. 'How are Amy and the cat getting along?' he said.

She looked up at him and he was rewarded with a faint smile. 'She loves that cat,' she said. 'It was so kind of Mr Barclay and you to think of giving it to her.'

They were approaching the gate of her house when she glanced at him again. 'I do hope Mr Barclay will be all right,' she said.

'How do you mean?' he prevaricated.

'Oh, I don't know. I guess I'm just being silly. All this trouble has made me nervous.'

They walked up the path and Jean brought out her key. 'Why don't you come in? I'll make some coffee.' As she opened the door they heard scratching sounds and the cat appeared.

'She's looking for Amy,' Jean said.

'She'll be back from school soon.'

Crawford leaned down and stroked the cat's fur. 'Thanks for the offer of some coffee,' he said, 'but if you don't mind I think I should maybe get back to work. I left the forge in a kind of a hurry.'

'Well, if you need to get back, I quite understand. You're welcome to come over any time.'

'That's real nice of you,' Crawford said. 'Are you sure you'll be all right? Make yourself some coffee and try to take it easy till Amy gets back.'

He satisfied himself that Jean was OK, then he waved to her as he went down the path and quickly made his way back to the forge. When he got there, however, he didn't stop. Instead he saddled up his horse and, settling into leather, began to ride hard along the stage route. He wanted to see for himself what had happened and to have a few words with the marshal.

As he rode he thought of Barclay and about recent events. His mind was far from clear, but he had a notion that it was time to take a stand against the gunslicks and hardcases who were causing such a degree of trouble. Barclay had shown the way. Maybe it was time to line up alongside him.

6

Barclay's eyes opened. He looked up at the rafters of a barn-like building. It was dim inside but when he raised his head and looked towards the entrance, some gleams of light filtered through a narrow crack beneath the door. His head felt fuzzy. He could hear a faint droning noise but he couldn't be sure whether it was in his head or if it came from outside. He guessed that he must have drifted into a troubled slumber. For a few moments he lay confused till his thoughts began to assemble. He was at the T Bench. He and Mulhall had been brought there the night before and locked in one of the outbuildings.

He looked round for Mulhall but couldn't see him. Assuming he must be just out of range, he made to get up from the iron bedstead on which he was lying but was immediately jerked back.

He felt a pain in his ankle and looked down. His leg was shackled to the bed by a chain, which ended in a heavy iron band that was locked about his leg just above the ankle. Raising himself up, he leaned forwards and attempted to free himself but he quickly realized it was useless. He sank back and took a further look about him. Apart from the bedstead on which he was lying, the barn was completely bare. It appeared almost as if it had been specifically designed for the purposes of incarcerating someone. The only window was a small opening high up one of the walls, way out of reach. As he considered his situation and what might have become of Mulhall, he began to feel thirsty. He hadn't eaten for a considerable time but it was the lack of water which affected him most. Would the gunslicks supply him with what he needed or did they just intend to leave him there, at least until their leader returned?

As he mulled over the matter, desperately casting about for some means of escape, he heard a noise and then the door swung open. Silhouetted against the light, a figure advanced into the room. It came forward and then stopped to retrace its footsteps. It closed the door and then advanced once again. Barclay felt peculiarly vulnerable and braced himself for what might be coming next, but before he could say anything himself, the other man spoke.

'Don't ask questions. We haven't got long. Just do as I say.' He sat down on the edge of the bed and, producing a key, proceeded to release Barclay's foot.

As soon as he was free Barclay stood up, almost toppling over as he did so. His foot felt numb. The shackle must have been fastened more tightly than he had realized. As feeling began to return to it, the numbness was succeeded by pangs of pins and needles. He shook his foot. While he did so the man handed him a gun. It was only then that he realized his own had been removed.

'Why are you doin' this?' he said. 'Who are you?'

'The name's Pym, but that's beside the point. The point is that we need to get out of here quick.'

Barclay's confused brain began to function. 'What about Mulhall?' he said.

'Mulhall?'

'The fella they brought in with me.'

'I thought I saw two of you,' Pym said. 'I figured the other man must be just another of Craven's gunslicks.'

'Like you?' Barclay interposed.

Pym looked at him. 'No, not like me.' He thought for a moment. 'I think I know Mulhall. I didn't recognize him in the dark. They must have put him somewhere else.'

'We've gotta find him.'

'I wouldn't argue with that.' Pym looked towards the doorframe. 'We haven't got much time,' he continued. 'I'm not sure what we do about Mulhall, but we need to get goin'. Trust me.'

Without further ado he moved to the door of the barn. Opening it a fraction, he peered out. 'OK,' he whispered. 'We're in luck. Let's go!' He opened the door wider and slipped through, followed by Barclay. The droning sound Barclay had heard inside became louder and, looking up, he saw the sails of the windmill revolving slowly in the breeze. Bowed low, they scuttled across a short stretch of ground to the shelter of the windmill.

'Chances are they've got Mulhall in one of the other outbuildings,' Pym continued. 'The question is; which one?' He turned a worried face to Barclay. 'Unless . . . '

'Those gunnies think I'm someone they have reason to keep alive, at least until Craven gets back. Mulhall's probably safe till then, too.'

'Why would they think that?' Pym said.

Barclay shrugged. 'I don't know. I guess there's only a few of the original gang still left.'

'So who do they think you are?'

'Someone by the name of Slessor.'

'Slessor! Not Frank Slessor? Not the Slessor who put Craven behind bars and split up the Splintered Canyon Bunch in the first place?'

'How do you know about that?'

'Then they *do* think you're Slessor!'

'Were you in the gang? I thought you just said you weren't one of them.'

'I'm not. In fact, I thought I'd already made it pretty plain that I don't like any of them. I don't like what's goin' on at the T Bench and I don't like what they've done to Miss Peyote.'

'Assumin' you're tellin' the truth and you really don't approve of what's been happenin', then now's your chance to do somethin' about it.'

Pym gave Barclay a steely glance. 'If I'm helpin' you now, it's because of Miss Peyote. I have every reason not to. In fact, I got every reason to want Slessor dead just as much as Craven. More than Craven. But Miss Peyote doesn't know what she's got herself into.'

It was Barclay's turn to give Pym a searching look. 'You're in love with Miss Peyote, aren't you?' he said.

Pym did not reply. Instead he turned his face away but Barclay could see his jaw working with the effort to contain his emotion. Suddenly he had an insight into the state of relations between Slessor and Miss Peyote.

'You hate Slessor because he and Miss Peyote were lovers,' he said. He used the past tense. From what he had seen of Slessor and Miss Peyote the night before, it seemed that it might still be the case. He didn't want to hurt Pym any further.

'You don't know anythin' about Slessor and Miss Peyote,' Pym said.

'I'm beginnin' to understand,' Barclay replied. He remembered how Slessor had been when he first found him. He recalled his lethargy, his reluctance to take action even though his own safety was in the balance.

'Slessor must have known Miss Peyote in the past. In fact — '

'Slessor was a member of the Splintered Canyon Bunch,' Pym burst out. 'They both were. When he broke with them, he tried to take Miss Peyote with him but it didn't work out that way. She went to the penitentiary with the rest of them.'

Things were becoming more and more transparent to Barclay. So that was why Slessor had been so lackadaisical. Miss Peyote had taken up again with Craven and his re-formed gang. The past had come back to haunt him. The easiest way was to give in to it. But it seemed that Miss Peyote had not behaved the way he had expected, or maybe the way she had expected either.

'Who is Miss Peyote?' he said.

Pym uttered a little, hollow laugh. 'Didn't you ever hear of Rosie Peyote? She once had something of a reputation. Before she teamed up with Craven she was involved with another gang down around the Rio Grande. Folks called them the Brownsville Bobcats. That's when I first knew her. I was one of them, too. In fact, I was rather more than just a member.'

'You mean . . . '

'Yeah. I was in love with Rosie Peyote even then. Of course, that's not her real name. I think it was more to do with the way she looked; kinda small and elusive, yet somehow powerful. Or maybe it was the effect she had on people.'

'And you're still holdin' a candle for her?'

'Yes, if you want to put it that way. And she ain't forgotten me. When she took over this place, she gave me a job. That was before Craven and his gang moved in again. But she stuck by me.'

Barclay was trying to assimilate what Pym was telling him and link it with his own intuitions.

'I hate Slessor,' Pym said. 'I don't know what she ever saw in him. I was the one who loved her. It was Slessor who betrayed her. When the Splintered Canyon Bunch attempted to rob the bank in Wister, the sheriff was ready for them. Most of the gang were killed and she ended up in the state pen. She came out quite a time ago but now it looks like she's in danger of gettin' back on the owlhoot trail. Unless I can stop her; unless I can prise her away from Craven.'

It was clear to Barclay that Pym found some measure of relief in talking about Miss Peyote. He had allowed him to run on but he was suddenly recalled to the perils of their situation by the sound of shouting coming from the direction of the bunkhouse. They both shrank back into the shadow of the windmill. A number of men appeared, running in the direction of the ranch house One of them was shouting: 'Prairie Dog! Prairie Dog!' as they vanished behind a corner of the building.

'Now what do you reckon that's all about?' Barclay said.

Before Pym could reply another figure burst through the door of the bunkhouse and began to run quickly in their direction. Barclay's gun sprang into his hand but then he recognized the running figure as Mulhall, rapidly pursued by a couple of gunnies. One of them had a revolver in his hand and raising it, he fired a shot at the fast-moving newspaper man. Mulhall was weaving from side to side and the bullet passed harmlessly by him. He was looking round for a means of escape when Barclay stepped out of cover.

'Over here!' he yelled. At the same moment his gun spat lead and the man who had fired the shot at Mulhall reeled backwards and sank to the floor. The other man turned and sprang back to the shelter of the bunkhouse. Mulhall's pace momentarily slackened and the next moment he was standing beside Barclay and Pym, panting for breath.

'Barclay!' he gasped. 'How did you escape?' His glance fell on the other man.

'Pym! Holy Moses, this just gets more

confusin'!' Before either Barclay or Pym could reply, a fusillade of shots rang out from the bunkhouse.

'We'll have to leave the explanations till later,' Barclay rapped. 'Right now we need to get out of here!'

Pym seemed to have a grasp on the situation. 'Quick!' he snapped. 'The stables are right behind. It's our only chance.'

Suiting action to his words, he turned towards the rear of the mill. At the same moment fresh shots began to ring out, this time from the ranch house. A short open space separated the windmill from the stable. Pym was across it in a flash, followed closely by Barclay and Mulhall.

Inside the stable a number of horses were stamping restlessly in their stalls. Saddles were hanging from pegs on the wall and it didn't take any time to throw them over the horses' backs. Quickly they tightened the cinches as shots continued to ring out, thudding into the wooden walls.

'Out the back way!' Pym shouted.

They led the horses out of the stable and quickly mounted. Fortunately, the stable building cut them off from the shooting, which had now built to a crescendo, but as they rode away they were exposed to it. They dug in their spurs and lay low along the horses' backs to reduce the risk of taking a hit. Bullets whined over their heads and raised plumes of dust around them but the horses ploughed on and they were soon out of range. Any thoughts that they were also out of danger were soon dispelled, however, as they glanced behind them to see that a number of the gunslicks had already mounted and were riding in hot pursuit.

Barclay was more concerned than the other two. They had had no opportunity to be selective in their choice of horses and it was a good bet that the gunslicks would have better mounts and be able to outride them.

As their horses plunged on, he looked about him for the best place to aim for.

He searched for cover and a position that would give them any kind of advantage but nothing presented itself. Gunfire was ringing out behind them but for the moment they didn't have too much to fear as they were out of range. He glanced back again over his shoulder. A group of the gunnies were bunched together but the others had begun to spread out in order to try and outflank them. Despite the pressing danger of their situation, he couldn't help wondering what had happened back at the bunkhouse when the gunslicks had rushed out calling for Prairie Dog. Had Mulhall something to do with that? Had he attempted to break free and caused the commotion or had something else happened, something of which he had then taken advantage? The latter seemed the likeliest scenario. So what had caused the disturbance?

They carried on riding at a furious pace for a little while longer, but Barclay knew they couldn't keep it up indefinitely. The horses were rapidly tiring and Craven's gunslicks were slowly but surely closing on them. He was desperately trying to come up with an answer to their predicament when he saw ahead of them a line of trees, indicating the course of a stream. If they could get into the brush they might have a chance. He pointed in the direction of the trees and shouted at the top of his voice. Whether they heard him or not he couldn't be sure, but they seemed to understand his meaning because they veered in the direction he indicated.

The horses were really struggling now. They were breathing hard and flecks of foam were flying from their nostrils. Barclay took another glance back and took heart from the fact that the gunslicks were still some way behind. If anything, they had increased their lead. Maybe he had been wrong about the horses; perhaps they were more rested than he'd thought. Certainly it was fortunate that Pym and

Mulhall both seemed to be good riders.

Despite the speed at which they were galloping, the line of trees seemed to come no closer. Barclay had the same sort of sensation he had experienced in dreams, of being entangled in something which held him back and prevented him from making any progress. The wind in his face and the steady drumming of their horses' hoofs told him otherwise, though; suddenly the trees were close and then they had ridden into them. Branches tore at their faces as they rode on to the banks of the stream and entered the water. They crossed to the other side where the banks were steeper.

'OK!' Barclay yelled. 'This is as good a place as any!'

They dropped to the ground and led the horses to a place of comparative safety among the trees before taking up a position overlooking the stream. They had a clear view and were well protected by the undergrowth. All in all, it was about the best they could have hoped for. Barclay's main wish was that they had rifles but they could be thankful that they at least possessed handguns. Barclay didn't know where Mulhall had acquired his; presumably he had wrested it from one of the gunnies when he made his break.

They had barely established themselves when they heard the hoofbeats of their pursuers. A few moments later the first rider appeared through the trees. Mulhall raised his gun but Barclay held up his hand for him to hold his fire. The rider spurred his horse through the trees and as he entered the water some of his fellows appeared behind him. Barclay's hand dropped and in the ensuing burst of gunfire the front rider toppled from his horse into the stream and one of the others behind him also fell. The third rider clutched at his shoulder but succeeded in holding on. He attempted to turn his horse but wasn't quick enough to avoid Barclay's next shot, which finally ripped him from the saddle. There were shouts from the following riders and from what Barclay could see, it appeared that they had taken the warning and spread out, reining back from making themselves a target. Barclay's keen eyes spotted movement among the trees and he loosed a few shots but he wasn't confident that they had found their mark. In a few moments bullets began to slice into the trees around them, tearing off leaves and branches and shards of bark.

'Why don't we move back?' Pym said.

'Better stay where we are. We've got plenty of cover and if anyone attempts to cross the stream, we'll have him in our sights.' Some of the shots were getting closer but on the whole the enemy fire was wayward.

'How many do you think there are?' Mulhall said.

'There was quite a bunch of 'em following us.'

'Let's hope they don't bring up reinforcements,' Pym replied.

Barclay turned to Mulhall. 'What happened back there in the bunkhouse?' he said.

'I'm not sure. It seems like it was somethin' to do with Miss Peyote. The gunnies started talkin' about her and got to speculatin' where she was. I guess they thought she was somewhere around the ranch house. Then someone joined in and said he'd seen her leave the T Bench with a man late the previous night. Looks like we weren't the only ones. That seemed to set them off. There was a bit of a hullabaloo. In the confusion I took my chance.'

'They'd put you in the bunkhouse?'

'Yeah, but they didn't seem to pay me a lot of attention. I reckon they clean forgot about me when the business about Miss Peyote suddenly blew up.' Barclay glanced at Pym. If he felt agitated, he didn't show it.

There was no chance to pursue the conversation as a fresh outburst of gunfire suddenly boomed out. They had reloaded their six-guns while they were talking and settled themselves to find targets. The gunfire roared again but it didn't seem to be coming from the opposite side of the river; it was hard to locate just exactly where it originated. Barclay and his companions exchanged glances. Had Prairie Dog brought up reinforcements as they had feared? As if in answer to his unspoken question there were indications of movement from the other side of the stream and presently Barclay glimpsed riders moving through the trees. They were further downriver and pretty well out of range of handguns. Mulhall fired a couple of shots but Barclay shook his head.

'Hold your fire,' he said. 'We might need all our bullets if they decide to rush us.' In the ensuing silence they heard the sound of hoofbeats and then there was another fusillade of shots. The hoofbeats began to fade.

'I'm not sure what's goin' on,' Barclay said. 'But I figure those varmints are leavin'.'

A few final shots rang out and then

there was silence. Mulhall made to move but Barclay indicated for him to stay where he was. 'Better not take any chances,' he said. 'It could be some kind of a ruse.' They remained in concealment, searching the brush on the opposite bank, listening for any sounds. Suddenly a voice rang out.

'Barclay! Is that you? It's Slessor. I'm comin' down the stream.'

'Slessor!' Barclay called back. He didn't know what to add. Instead, he watched the stream and was soon rewarded by the sight of two riders splashing their way through the shallow water. The first was Slessor but he didn't recognize the one behind. It was Pym who suddenly cried out: 'Miss Peyote!'

'It's OK,' Barclay said to reassure the others. 'That's my friend Slessor.' He rose to his feet and slithered down the bank so that he was standing in the water. Mulhall and Pym followed him. The two riders approached at a steady pace and when they were close, Slessor jumped down.

'Barclay! It's sure good to see you!'

Barclay was still too surprised by his friend's unexpected appearance to say anything. The next moment Slessor had reached him and they were locked in an embrace. Pulling back, Slessor moved to the other horse and helped its rider to dismount. She was dressed in range gear but there was no mistaking her good looks and the roundness of her figure.

'Barclay,' Slessor said, 'let me introduce you to Miss Rosie Peyote. Rosie, this is my good friend Jet Barclay.' The lady held out her hand and Barclay took it.

'It's nice to meet you, Mr Barclay,' she said. 'Frank has spoken of you.' She glanced at Pym and acknowledged him with a nod of her head.

'We figured you were in a spot of trouble,' Slessor said, 'but I guess we just struck lucky the way those gunnies rode off. They couldn't have known there were only two of us.'

'They'll probably be back,' Barclay said.

'They'll certainly be back,' Miss Peyote interposed, 'which is why we need to work out just what we intend to do.'

'Isn't she great?' Slessor said. 'Nothin' fazes her.'

She turned to Slessor and smiled. 'Not any more,' she said softly.

'Where are your horses?' Slessor said.

'Back in the trees.'

'Then let's fetch 'em and get out of here.'

'There's an old cabin about half a dozen miles away,' Miss Peyote said. 'We'll head for it.'

Barclay wondered if she and Slessor had spent the night there. He took another glance at Pym. He seemed to be OK but there was no mistaking the state of play between Slessor and Miss Peyote. It seemed to him that the situation could get awkward but there was nothing to be done about it.

Without saying anything further, they made their way through the trees to where the horses were tethered and climbed into leather.

'Follow me,' Miss Peyote said. She took the lead and they followed, Slessor right behind her and Pym bringing up the rear.

* * *

By the time Crawford arrived at the scene of the stagecoach robbery and massacre, the marshal had already carried out his investigations. He was standing by the horses, wiping his brow with his bandanna, when the black-smith rode up.

'You're takin' somethin' of a risk, Crawford,' he said. 'It's just as well I'm not the jumpy sort or I might have figured you were one of the varmints who did this.'

'I heard about it back at the depot,' Crawford replied. 'Jean Sandoz was pretty cut up about it.'

'She had good cause,' the marshal replied. 'Take a look for yourself.'

Crawford dismounted and did as the marshal suggested. The sight was a sickening one, even for someone as hardened by experience as himself. When he had seen all he needed, he approached the marshal.

'Have you any ideas about who's responsible?' he said. The marshal looked at him quizzically.

'Why?' he replied. 'Have you?'

'Matter of fact, yes I do.'

'And would it be the same varmints I got in mind?'

'There's been a lot of trouble recently, one way and another,' Crawford replied. 'It's fairly common knowledge that a lot of it stems from some of those no-good *hombres* who profess to ride for the T Bench. I figure that's where we look for the culprits.'

The marshal put his bandanna in his pocket. 'Now ain't that a coincidence,' he said. 'That's just what I've been thinkin'. Maybe I should have done somethin' more about it before now. I sure don't intend lettin' anyone get away with this.'

'Are you thinkin' of organizin' a posse?' Crawford inquired. The marshal regarded him closely.

'I might,' he said. 'On the other hand, that would take time and what have we got to go on apart from our own instincts?'

'You might need some help,' Crawford said.

The marshal regarded him closely. 'I gather you had some contact with a fella by name of Barclay.'

Crawford nodded. 'How do you know about him?' he asked.

'Oh, I keep my ear to the ground. Apart from that, he got involved in a spot of bother with a couple of the gunslicks. I know. I saw the bodies.'

'Barclay seems to have some sort of score to settle.'

'Did he mention the Splintered Canyon Bunch?'

'I don't know. He might have.'

'It don't matter. Let's just say I reckon there's more goin' on here than the fact that some hard-cases have somehow got involved with the T Bench. Anyone taking them on is gonna be invitin' a whole heap of trouble.'

'Are you tryin' to warn me off or somethin'?' Crawford said.

'I ain't intendin' to waste time roundin' up no posse. But like you say, I might need some help.'

The blacksmith's face creased in a broad grin. 'I got my rifle and six-guns right with me,' he said.

'Then why wait around? I already arranged for the undertaker to come out before I left town. He'll take care of things here.'

'OK,' Crawford replied. 'Let's make for the T Bench.'

★ ★ ★

Jean Sandoz stood by the window and watched her daughter play with the cat. Unconsciously, her face broke into a gentle smile. Seeing Amy made her feel better. After Crawford left she had felt really nervous and upset, although she had tried not to show too much of it to the blacksmith. Just lately it seemed as if things had gone wrong with the world and she had seen an aspect of it of which she had never been aware before. The town had changed from being a friendly, comfortable community to being a place of danger and disquiet. The trampling to death of the old cat had brought it all home in a peculiarly personal way and now the stagecoach robbery and murders had made it all horribly real again.

For the first time in a long while she had taken a drink but it was only the return of Amy from school that had helped calm her. As she watched her, she felt the familiar world restored. Crawford was part of that world, and the marshal, and now Barclay. Barclay might be a newcomer, but already she felt drawn to him and comfortable in his presence. She was conscious of feelings she hadn't experienced since the death of her husband and she wasn't sure what to make of them. Was she being foolish? Would the safest thing be to put Barclay out of her thoughts? But she had tried that and it didn't work. What was he doing now? Would she see him again?

After a time she turned aside and made her way into the kitchen. It would soon be time for Amy's tea. The best way to deal with the thoughts and impressions that were swimming about in her brain was to be practical; she needed to be doing things to occupy herself. That was the way she had coped in the past and it was the way she would get through now. She began to busy herself, pausing every now and again to glance through the doorway at her daughter. It was good of Barclay to have given Amy the cat. It was reassuring to think of him. It would be even more reassuring to have him beside her.

7

The little group of riders led by Miss Peyote soon arrived at the cabin of which she had spoken. It didn't amount to much but even so Barclay had the impression that it wasn't entirely deserted. There were curtains at the window, partly drawn, and a couple of chairs stood on the porch. His keen eyes detected traces of hoofprints in the ground nearby. When the door was opened and they passed inside, his impressions were confirmed. The remains of a fire stood in the grate and an old settee bore the imprint of having been recently sat on. On a shelf at the back stood a number of tins of foodstuffs, coffee and some bottles. A door leading into a back room was closed and did not reveal its secrets. Barclay looked at Pym but he wasn't giving anything away.

'Better take the horses round the

back,' Miss Peyote said.

It seemed to Barclay that her speech was slightly strained. Was she feeling even a little awkward? He looked at her closely, trying to see in her some trace of the woman described by Pym, the woman who in her younger days had been a leading figure in the Brownsville Bobcats and Splintered Canyon Bunch. It was hard to believe but one thing was certain: she was still a beauty and she held herself with an air of assurance. She was clearly not someone to mess with.

'I'll see to the horses,' Barclay volunteered. He wanted to see what the set-up was like. He led the horses round the side of the shack. There was a partially fenced area of grass at the back beyond which was a stand of trees and he picketed them there. Then he made his way to the trees and began to make his way through them. They didn't extend very far but when he reached the edge of the wooded patch he drew up in surprise. He had expected a further stretch of open country but instead the land fell away quite abruptly into a wide canyon beyond which he was surprised to see the outline of Horned Toad Head. He was looking at it from a different angle and it presented a different appearance, but all the same he recognized it. He strained his eyes to see if he could detect the cattle pen and buildings lying in its shadow but they were either too far away or obscured by the angle of the cliff. When he had satisfied himself as to the lie of the land, he made his way back to the cabin.

As he came through the door, it was clear that preparations for a meal had already commenced. Only then did he notice that he was hungry. He had lost track of time but now realized that it must be well into the afternoon. He and Mulhall had been brought to the T Bench in the small hours of the previous night. He didn't know how long he had been locked in the outbuilding shackled to the bed frame, but a lot of things had happened since Pym had appeared; a fair amount of time must have passed. He was still in a state of confusion about their situation, and in particular about what had happened to Slessor and what was going on between him and Miss Peyote. It was decidedly awkward that they were all pitched in together. He would have liked to speak to Slessor alone but there didn't seem to be much chance of that.

'You took the opportunity to take a good look at the place?' Miss Peyote remarked when he entered the cabin.

'Yeah. Always pays to know the lie of the country,' he replied.

'Do you think we're doing the right thing setting ourselves up here?'

'There's nowhere else to run,' he answered.

'Who's running?'

He gave her a searching glance. 'Are you sure you know which side you're on?' he said. It was a dangerous question but she didn't appear to be put out by it.

'I know which side I'm on,' she replied, glancing in the direction of Slessor. 'Now.'

Barclay was still confused about her role in respect of the T Bench. If she was in cahoots with Craven and his gang — and he was finding it hard to think otherwise — she had pretty soon changed her mind. Could the short space of time she had spent with Slessor be sufficient to account for it? He had a feeling that he was out of his depth. He found himself once again thinking of Jean Sandoz. Now there was a woman and a situation he could understand. And there was no mystery about the state of his feelings for her. He had come to Wind Creek to sort out the trouble that had brewed there and then find himself a place to settle down. He hadn't expected to find someone to settle down with. The thought of her brought a sense of calmness and relief. It was like finding a cool clear stream in a fevered landscape. He suddenly realized that there was no way he was going to let her go.

* * *

Ral Craven and his gang of murderers and thieves arrived back at the T Bench still in a state of jubilation at the success of their attack on the stage-coach. They rode into the yard expecting to be met by Prairie Dog and the rest of the boys, but the place was strangely quiet. Some of the horses in the corral showed signs of having been recently ridden. Craven sensed that something was not quite right and his suspicions were confirmed when Prairie Dog appeared on the veranda. Craven swung down from his horse. 'You look like you lost a dollar and found a cent,' he remarked.

Prairie Dog attempted a grin but only succeeded in grimacing. 'Looks like you boys were successful,' he replied.

'We sure were. We got the strongbox

— it was easy.' Craven turned to his men. 'Somebody carry that thing in here. The rest of you get on over to the bunkhouse and make yourselves comfortable.'

He strode through the door of the ranch house and made his way to the drinks cabinet. He poured himself a stiff drink while his henchman carried in the strongbox and then left. Craven swallowed a mouthful of whiskey before addressing Prairie Dog, who had followed him inside.

'You'd better tell me what's happened,' he said. He looked around. 'Where's Miss Peyote? I figured she'd be here to welcome me back.'

Prairie Dog looked uncomfortable. 'Miss Peyote's gone,' he said.

'Gone?'

'It seems she slipped away last night. One of the boys saw her leave.'

'What are you talkin' about? Where would she go?'

'I don't know. Apparently there was someone with her.'

Craven's expression was a mixture of anger, confusion and disbelief. 'You'd better explain just what you mean.'

Prairie Dog gave a high-pitched cough to clear his throat. 'It's like this,' he began. He hesitated, not knowing just where to start. Then he coughed once more and, seeing the increasing look of exasperation on Craven's face, launched into his account of what had taken place. When he had finished Craven's reaction was to hurl the glass that he had emptied against the wall.

'You had Slessor and you let him go?' he fulminated.

'We had him chained up. I can't figure out how he managed to get away.'

'I'd say that was pretty obvious. You just said that Pym was involved.'

'Yes but — '

'I don't want to hear your excuses!' Craven thundered. He swore loudly and then, grabbing the bottle, poured more liquor down his throat. Prairie Dog waited a moment for Craven's initial burst of fury to subside before attempting to pacify him.

'It ain't as bad as it seems,' he said.

'How do you make that out? I'd say it was about as bad as it gets.'

'We know where Slessor's hiding. Pym's there with him. So is Miss Peyote and the fella she rode off with. They're at the old line shack.'

'I don't get this. What's Miss Peyote doin' there? And who is this other fella?'

'I don't know. But there's only five of 'em.'

'Five? I thought you just mentioned four.'

'There's the one we brought in with Slessor.'

Craven began to stomp up and down the carpet. 'Five of the varmints,' he said. 'And you couldn't handle 'em. Well, it should be easy enough to deal with them now. If they're still where you say they are.'

'They're there. I got a couple of the boys keepin' an eye on things.'

'You'd better be right.' Craven scratched at his ear. 'Me and the boys have been doin' some ridin',' he said. 'I could do with somethin' to eat. Once we've had a chance to take a little rest we'll set out for the line shack. Round up all the boys and tell 'em to get ready to ride.'

'Sure,' Prairie Dog replied. He started for the door.

'Remember,' Craven called, 'I still want Slessor alive.' He thought for a moment. 'And that goes for Miss Peyote, too. I can't believe how you managed to make such a mess of things, but I'm takin' charge now.'

'Yes,' Prairie Dog squeaked. 'Don't worry. They can't get away. They caught us on the hop once but things are different now you're here.'

'Get the cook to rustle somethin' up,' Craven said. 'And you can clear up that broken glass, too.'

$\star \quad \star \quad \star$

The marshal and Crawford rode steadily in the direction of the T Bench. They had both fallen silent, each of them thinking about what they had witnessed at the scene of the stagecoach robbery. They were thinking, too, of what they might find when they got to the T Bench.

The marshal had met Miss Peyote before but he didn't know how far she was implicated in the various incidents that had marred the smooth running of his town and spilled over into the nearby settlement of Wind Creek. He had no other plan in mind than to speak to her and try to find out just what was going on at the T Bench. He knew that she had been fencing in her land but he was still somewhat surprised to see how far the work had progressed. Maybe that wasn't just Miss Peyote's decision: it seemed to be the way the open range was going. One thing was for sure: barbed wire and fence posts cost money and it took considerable labour to erect them. Miss

Peyote didn't seem to be short of capital. He noted, too, the increased number of stock. The T Bench appeared to be thriving. Miss Peyote had sold part of the land on which the new cattle pens had been erected, but he had heard it was for a reduced figure. What money she had acquired from that deal didn't seem to account for her obvious outgoings. And she seemed to have taken on a lot of ranch-hands — if that was the right word to use in connection with most of the men she employed.

'We'd better be careful from now on in,' he said to Crawford.

'You figure Craven will come out fightin'?'

'He ain't gonna take any notice of this badge, if that's what you mean,' Crawford grinned.

'I guess there ain't much chance of that.'

'It depends to some extent on Miss Peyote and on what sort of influence she has over those gunslingin' varmints.'

'Seems like they work for her.'

'Sure. They might be takin' her orders now, but if things get hot, they might see things differently.'

'Especially if this *hombre* Craven is involved.'

'Yeah. So I guess we'll just have to play it by ear.'

Touching their spurs to the horses' flanks, they rode on towards the T Bench.

★　★　★

Daybreak arrived and found the occupants of the line cabin preparing for the attack they were certain was about to come from Craven and his gunslicks. From what Prairie Dog had said, they knew that Craven and the rest of the gang were expected back at the T Bench and it seemed just a question of whether Prairie Dog would wait till his return or launch the attack himself. The fact that Prairie Dog had led his men back to the T Bench after the affair at the stream suggested that he was playing safe but also that Craven's arrival was imminent.

Barclay had had no opportunity to speak with Slessor. The previous night's conversation had skirted around anything awkward and concentrated instead on how they should deal with the threat from Craven.

'I wonder what kind of business took him away from the T Bench,' Mulhall remarked.

'I don't know, but you can sure bet it wasn't anythin' good.'

'He's obviously not content with just stealin' cattle,' Mulhall replied.

'Once an outlaw, always an outlaw,' Barclay said. 'He's got a perfect set-up here between the T Bench and the cattle-shipping operation, but he isn't content with that.'

'Strange. He obviously has a certain business sense but, like you say, it ain't enough.'

'I guess he's also out to prove a point,' Barclay replied.

'How do you mean?'

'Well, look at the way he came after Slessor. The fact that Slessor was responsible for the death of his brother and for puttin' him in jail must have rankled with him all the time he was behind bars. Once he got out, the first thing he did was to hit the owlhoot trail and go after Slessor.'

'I can't quite figure Miss Peyote out. You figure she's in with Craven?'

Barclay glanced round. Miss Peyote seemed to have done a good job of stage-managing things so that none of the awkward questions had arisen. For the moment he couldn't see her.

'Apparently Miss Peyote and Slessor go way back,' he said.

'Yeah? I ain't surprised. I kinda figured that.'

'My guess is that Miss Peyote got involved with Craven, probably against her better judgement. Maybe Craven installed her on the T Bench, but I'd say it was more likely she already had this place. Craven saw how it might have its uses. He bought some of the land off her and built those cattle pens.'

Just then the door of the cabin opened and Miss Peyote herself emerged. Just behind her came Slessor.

'You boys figurin' how best to hold off Craven when he comes this way? I thought we'd already decided that last night,' said Miss Peyote.

'Just checkin' the terrain.'

'You seem to make a habit of that.'

'I don't think we should abandon the cabin,' Mulhall said.

'Believe me, I know what I'm talking about,' Miss Peyote replied.

'Miss Peyote's right,' Barclay said. 'We don't want to get bogged down in the cabin. Those trees should give us sufficient cover.'

'If the worst comes to the worst, and things get sticky, Miss Peyote knows a way down into the canyon,' Slessor interjected.

Miss Peyote smiled at them. 'Come with me,' she said. 'I'll show you.' She made to move away when Slessor held up his hand.

'Listen!' he rapped. They stopped in their tracks and held their breath. From some distance away they could hear the faint drumming of hoofbeats.

'Looks like they're on their way,' Barclay said. 'Let's get into the woods.'

It took no time to do so. Once they had taken cover, they listened as the sound of approaching hoofs grew louder and louder. A thick pall of dust hung in the air; it was clear that Craven and his gang were coming in numbers. Barclay was beginning to have second thoughts about the wisdom of standing and fighting. Maybe it would have been more sensible to cut and run. However, whether it was right or wrong, the decision had been made and they had to stand by it.

They were well sheltered by the trees and he took comfort from the fact that they had a line of retreat. At least, Miss Peyote had assured him, there was a trail down into the canyon. She had not had time to show it to the rest of them but presumably she knew what she was talking about. He was confident that they would put up a good show. He had no fears for Slessor or Mulhall and Miss Peyote herself had shown every indication of being a woman who had ridden the outlaw trail in the past.

Pym had remained silent and withdrawn. Barclay had a feeling that he was beyond caring what happened to him. He had been forced to acknowledge that Miss Peyote was beyond his reach; he had probably never thought otherwise. Still, following Slessor's appearance on the scene, his position had been made abundantly evident.

The drumming of hoofs sounded like overhead thunder. From his angle of vision, Barclay had a clear view of the front yard. He expected to see the open space fill with men and horses but the clatter of hoofs drew to a stop without anyone appearing. There was a babble of voices and it was obvious that at least some of the riders were dismounting.

Evidently, Craven was unwilling to carry on riding right up to the cabin; he knew he couldn't be certain about what sort of reception he might receive. They didn't have long to wait, however, before a voice came ringing through the air.

'This is Ral Craven! It's Slessor we want! Hand him over and the rest of you can go free.'

Barclay looked towards the others. For the first time he noticed that Slessor and Miss Peyote were missing. He assumed they had changed position and were obscured by some of the vegetation. The last echoes of the voice dwindled away and the silence seemed heavy by contrast. After a few more moments it rang out again.

'Slessor! Have you got Miss Peyote in there? If so, why don't you let her go?'

Barclay shifted uneasily. He still couldn't see either Miss Peyote or Slessor. The shadow of a doubt began to steal across his mind. Had Slessor and Miss Peyote made their getaway?

Had they gone off together again? But if so, why had they bothered to come to the rescue of himself, Pym and Mulhall only the day before? He had no time for further considerations as the voice called again.

'This is the last warnin'! If Slesssor ain't out in five minutes, we're comin' on in!'

Barclay took another look towards where the others had concealed themselves. Pym and Mulhall had their rifles at the ready but still he could see no sign of Slessor or Miss Peyote. He was racking his brains trying to think of the best way to respond to Craven's challenge. In five minutes Craven's men would open fire. They would soon realize that the cabin was deserted. When they came out into the open, that would be the time to return fire. Five minutes. Just enough time to slink back among the trees and see if he could locate Slessor. Signalling to the others, he began to move backwards when his attention was drawn to the roof of the cabin; Slessor had appeared on it. Barclay gasped. His friend was fully exposed. He must have gone crazy to make himself such an easy target. At any moment Barclay expected his friend to be shot down but nothing happened. He glanced at the others. They had seen Slessor and were staring open-mouthed at the spectacle.

'I'm right here, Craven!' Slessor shouted. There was an answering cry, but it wasn't what Barclay had expected.

'Don't shoot!' Craven called. For a moment Barclay misunderstood what he meant till he realized that the words were aimed not at Slessor but at his own men. Then he recalled some words Slessor had once spoken, about his hunch that Craven would want to savour his revenge. He suddenly understood why Slessor had not gone down in a hail of bullets. He also knew on how thin a thread Slessor's life hung. It would only take one of the gunnies to forget or to have an itchy trigger finger for Slessor to die. Just then Slessor spoke again.

'Craven! I got support and we got your men covered. If you go ahead with this a lot of people are goin' to die. So why don't you and I settle this between us? There's no need for anyone else to get hurt.' He paused but there was no immediate response.

'Craven! You hear me? I'll get down from here and meet you out in the open. Just you and me. Man to man. What do you say?'

The words seemed to hang in the air. Barclay certainly wasn't expecting any response from Craven. Then, to his surprise, the figure of a man impinged itself on his vision. The man walked slowly forward for a few steps and then stopped.

'OK, Slessor. Here I am. Now why don't you get down off that roof like you say.'

Barclay glanced up at the roof. It was low and already Slessor had swung his legs over the edge. For a moment he disappeared from Barclay's view as he dropped to the ground but seconds later he reappeared in front of the building.

'One thing, Craven,' he said.

'Yeah? What's that?'

'You chose this. I didn't. But I aim to end it once and for all. Get ready to join your brother.'

Although he was some distance away, Barclay could sense Craven's anger. He also recognized another of Slessor's old tricks. The words he had spoken had been nicely calculated to unsettle his opponent. There was no doubt in Barclay's mind that Slessor himself was as cold as ice.

'You dirty swine!' Craven expostulated.

'What's more, I got Miss Peyote. I guess you could say you were the one to bring us together.'

His comment made Barclay wonder whether Craven had been another of Miss Peyote's admirers but he didn't pursue the thought. It was of no concern either way and Slessor's words were more likely to be just another ploy to unnerve his opponent. One thing Barclay couldn't work out was why Craven seemed to have accepted Slessor's challenge. A glint of sunlight glancing off something metallic reminded him of the answer: Craven's men had him covered. It would never get as far as a final shootout between him and Slessor. Unless . . .

Where was Miss Peyote?

Almost as quickly as the thought crossed his mind, he saw a plume of smoke rise into the air somewhere to the rear of Craven. He would have noticed it earlier if he hadn't confused it with the remnants of the dust cloud raised by Craven and his horsemen. In a few moments tongues of flame began to appear. So far Craven hadn't noticed anything but a gathering wave of noise behind him made him realize something was amiss. He turned, confused, but was arrested in his tracks by the voice of Slessor.

'Face up, Craven! Or are you too scared?'

Craven swung back. His face was livid with fury and twisted with hate. His hand dropped to his holster and in a fraction of time his six-gun was in his hand and spitting lead. Quick as he was, Slessor was quicker. His first shot caught Craven in the shoulder, jerking him backwards, causing Slessor to miss with the next shot. Slessor took a step to the side and fired again. For a moment Barclay thought that he had missed for the second time and he watched as if frozen as Craven raised his gun. Before Craven's finger could close on the trigger, however, he took a wavering step forwards and then another before collapsing face forward to the ground.

Barclay had watched the rapidly unfolding events as if temporarily stupefied but he was jerked back to the moment as a burst of gunfire rang out, aimed not at the cabin but at where he and the others were waiting in the trees.

They had obviously been detected. Bullets whipped and whined among the branches overhead. Jerked into action, Barclay began to return fire. Stabs of flame on either side told him that Pym and Mulhall had opened fire, too. A branch torn from the tree behind which he had been hiding landed on his head and knocked him to the ground. He couldn't see what had happened between Slessor and Craven and had no time to do anything further as a furious hail of bullets ripped into the brush. A barrage of sound assailed his ears; the boom of gunfire, men shouting, the bray of horses and the thunder of their hoofs, the crackling of flames. It was clear to him that there were more of the gunslicks than he had reckoned for and that the conflagration started by Miss Peyote was only going to go a little way towards defeating them. Bullets were raining in now from all sides and it seemed the outlaws were gaining the upper hand. His head hurt and blood was flowing down his face. He glanced about him. Mulhall and Pym were still firing back at the gunslicks but it seemed it must be only a question of time till they were overrun.

His fears seemed to be confirmed when he heard footsteps behind him. Quickly he turned but instead of the sight of encroaching gunnies meeting his eye, it was Miss Peyote. Slessor emerged just behind her. Barclay was about to speak when Miss Peyote silenced him.

'This is no time for questions,' she said. 'Just follow me.'

Slessor signalled to the others and in another few moments they had all begun to slither their way through the trees. The fusillade of firing and the lurid flicker of flames followed them through the woods. They emerged into the open and found themselves at the edge of the canyon. There seemed to be no way of escape but Miss Peyote beckoned them. Quickly, taking advantage of the temporary shelter provided by the wall of trees, they moved along the lip of the plateau till Miss Peyote paused and pointed. About twelve feet below was a slight ledge.

'You will need to take care,' she said. 'Watch me.'

Without further ado she sat down and began to lower herself over the rim, clinging on with her fingers. When she had gone as far as she dared, she let go. The drop was still significant and she landed quite heavily. Barclay's heart was in his mouth. It seemed that she must topple over the ledge but somehow she held firm and with a forward movement succeeded in steadying herself against the wall of the cliff. Barclay glanced at Slessor. Anxiety was written across his features.

Miss Peyote's voice sounded from below. 'Quickly, before Craven's boys get here.'

Barclay turned to the others. 'Who wants to go next?' he said.

Before anyone could reply there was

a hail of gunfire from the trees and a group of gunslicks burst into the open. Without hesitation Barclay and his companions dropped to their knees and opened fire. Three of the gunnies fell but even as they did so more of the owlhoots began to emerge at different points.

'Take cover!' Barclay shouted.

They rolled behind some rocks as lead began to pour down on them. Pym winced and a dark stain appeared on the lower part of his trousers.

'Have you been hit?' Barclay said. Pym nodded.

'I'll be OK,' he replied.

Slessor was nearest to him and, taking his bandanna from his neck, he made to wrap it round Pym's upper leg. Pym pushed him aside.

'Get your hands off me,' he said. Slessor looked at him curiously.

'What's eatin' you?' he said. Barclay was too busy occupied with repelling the sudden influx of gunnies to intervene, but when he had the opportunity to take another look he could see that Pym's face was twisted with emotion. He couldn't tell to what extent it was due to the pain in his leg and how much was an expression of his hatred for Slessor. Suddenly Pym rose to his feet.

'Stay put!' Barclay shouted.

Pym raised his rifle and for an awful moment Barclay thought he was going to aim it at Slessor. Instead he turned and began to walk towards the oncoming gunslicks. Shots rained around him but he appeared to lead a charmed life. Raising his weapon, he fired rapidly on the outlaws. Barclay and his companions watched in horror but they had sufficient presence of mind to try and support the staggering figure of Pym with a covering fire. Pym stumbled on, continuing to shoot till his rifle was out of bullets, when he flung it from him.

The gunslicks seemed to have become preoccupied with something to their rear. All of them except one, who advanced to the rim of the canyon and drew a bead on the figure of Miss Peyote, still sheltering on the ledge below.

'Hold it right there, Prairie Dog!' Pym shouted.

The little man hesitated for a moment before tightening his finger on the trigger. As the gun exploded, Pym flung himself into the firing line. Prairie Dog didn't wait; leaping to his feet, he began to run for the trees. He didn't make it. A rattle of fire from the woods beyond caught him and sent him crashing to the ground. A couple of gunnies who still remained were aiming in the direction from which the shots had come. Through the haze of gunsmoke, Barclay caught a glimpse of a couple of figures who were continuing to fire at Craven's men.

'Who the hell could that be?' Slessor hissed.

'I don't know, but I'm sure glad they turned up.'

The volume of fire had decreased and it seemed that the gunnies were discouraged by the sudden turn of events. They began to retreat into the trees. Barclay directed his attention back to Pym. Blood was oozing from his chest and Barclay realized he must have taken the bullet meant for Miss Peyote. It was impossible to tell if he was badly hurt or not. Holding his hand to his chest, he began to walk back towards the others.

'Get down!' Barclay screamed.

Pym seemed to be oblivious to everything around him. He staggered on till he reached the point where Miss Peyote had lowered herself over the edge of the cliff. At that moment Slessor got to his feet and, leaping across the intervening gap, made to grab him by the arm to drag him back to safety. Pym pushed him off but Slessor held on. They fell back and for a moment tottered perilously on the rim of the cliff. Barclay got to his knees, intending to lend his support to Slessor, but before he could reach them Pym had torn himself from Slessor's grip. He swayed and then, with a final look at Miss Peyote, who still clung to the ledge below, his feet gave way and without a sound he went over the edge in a headlong fall to the canyon floor.

Slessor made a hopeless attempt to catch him before having to turn his attention to the gunnies as more shots tore up the earth beside him. It was their last throw of the dice. Caught between Barclay, Slessor and Mulhall and the hail of fire from the newcomers, and not knowing how many of them there might be, they began to retreat and make their way back through the trees.

Pausing only long enough to help drag Miss Peyote back to the top of the cliff, Barclay, Slessor and Mulhall set off in pursuit. When they emerged from the trees, it was apparent that they had no more to fear from the Splintered Canyon Bunch. Their numbers were sorely depleted; some had ridden away and only a few dispirited remnants remained. They were beaten and offered no further resistance. The scene was one of devastation, though by now the fire was beginning to burn itself out. Surprisingly, the cabin had not been touched.

When the last of the gunnies had surrendered their arms, the bushes parted and two figures emerged into the open. Barclay turned to them, not knowing what to expect. His face broke into an expression of amazement when he recognized Crawford and the marshal.

'Well I'll be ... ' he began but, unable to find the appropriate words, he gave up the attempt. Crawford came forward and they embraced. The marshal glanced at the few remaining sorry-looking gunslicks.

'Leave those varmints to me,' he said self-consciously. 'I'll make sure they face justice.'

'I don't know how, but you got here just at the right time,' Barclay said. He looked about him. 'I could sure use a drink,' he said, 'but I figure we got some tidyin' up to do first.'

★ ★ ★

It was late by the time they had finished. Miss Peyote, assisted by Mulhall, had prepared a good meal and they set to with a good appetite. Only the absence of Pym acted as a break on their high spirits. With some reluctance, Miss Peyote and Slessor had climbed down the narrow trail leading to the valley floor to seek Pym's body and make sure he was dead. It was Slessor's opinion that he had died before hitting the valley floor. Prairie Dog's bullet had gone straight to his heart.

'He was the hero,' Slessor said. 'If he hadn't have gotten in the way, that bullet would have hit Miss Peyote.'

'We can't be sure of that,' Barclay replied.

'I got a lot to thank Pym for,' Slessor said.

Mulhall had been listening from the kitchen where he was making coffee. 'I'll make sure his story is told,' he said. 'When I write this whole thing up for the *Clarion*, and folks know their troubles are over, it's going to make for quite an exclusive.'

'Just be a little discreet when it comes to some of the things you write,' Miss Peyote interjected.

Barclay had been hesitant about asking Slessor and Miss Peyote too many questions, but he needn't have been because they seemed happy to talk themselves.

'Sorry about that Wind Creek business,' Slessor said. 'Maybe I should have done what we agreed to when you left to go to Poverty, but when I picked up Craven's sign leading to the T Bench, I decided to follow it. When I got there he and his gang had already left. Instead I found Miss Peyote.'

'I'd never forgotten Slessor,' Miss Peyote said. 'At one point I blamed him for everything that happened to the Splintered Canyon Bunch and to me but I came to see that it wasn't his fault, that I wasn't being fair.'

'Did Craven set you up at the T Bench?' Craven asked.

'No. I bought the place myself. When Craven got back in touch with me, I wasn't too happy, but I didn't know what to do. I felt in a way I still owed him something. I couldn't see any objection to selling him part of the property. His scheme for setting up the cattle-shipping business seemed like a reasonable proposition. It was only gradually I came to see what he was up to. He moved his men in here. I should have done somethin' about it but I didn't. I guess I just sorta got sucked in.'

'I hadn't forgotten Miss Peyote either,' Slessor said. He gave a slightly embarrassed grin. 'Hell, how could I? It was her shot off part of my ear!'

'But you figured she still held a grudge and wouldn't forgive you,'

Barclay continued, ignoring Slessor's moment of levity. 'You figured she was still takin' an active part in the restored Splintered Canyon Bunch. That's another reason why you were so down when I found you.'

'Yeah. That's about the size of it. I got you to thank for helpin' me get back on my feet again.'

'What are you and Miss Peyote goin' to do now?' Barclay said.

'Well, I reckon you and me have done the first part of what we set out to do,' Slessor said. 'I figure we've just about rid both Poverty and Wind Creek of Craven and his gunnies. Now maybe it's time to get on with the second part and settle down.'

'On the T Bench?' Barclay said. Slessor and Miss Peyote both nodded.

'That's the way we figure it,' Slessor replied.

'But those fences are gonna be comin' down,' Miss Peyote interposed.

Barclay laughed. 'Isn't it funny,' he said. 'I came out here intendin' to buy a ranch and settle down, but Slessor's the one who does it.' Slessor looked slightly uncomfortable. 'What'll you do?' he asked.

Barclay thought of Jean Sandoz. 'I got some plans,' he said. 'Maybe I'd better tell you about what happened to me in Poverty.'

★   ★   ★

It was a sunny morning. Jean Sandoz sat in her garden watching Amy play with the cat. She had not been back to work since the stagecoach holdup but the shock she had felt at the time had subsided and she was in a reflective frame of mind. The whole affair had made her even more appreciative of her own situation. As long as she had Amy and a roof over her head, did she really need anything more? And yet she felt a strange emptiness. Inevitably her thoughts turned to Barclay. It was only since she had met him that she had begun to think that way.

Suddenly her reflections were interrupted by the sound of hoofbeats and, looking up, she saw a rider approaching. There was nothing particularly unusual about that and she was about to turn her head away when her heart seemed to skip a beat. The rider was Barclay. She jumped to her feet and ran down the path, reaching the gate as Barclay drew his horse to a halt and stepped down. He turned to her. For the barest fraction of a moment they both hesitated and then he had opened the gate and she was in his arms. He held her tight, not saying anything, and it was only when Amy ran up that he released her.

'Mr Barclay!' Amy said. 'Where have you been?'

Barclay looked down. 'How's Tabitha?' he said. 'I've missed you both.' They walked up the path, Barclay still holding Jean's hand, but they didn't immediately go inside. Instead they seated themselves on the chairs on the veranda, one of which Jean had just vacated. Amy sat on the step with the cat in her arms.

'Can we go for another buggy ride?' she asked.

'Give Mr Barclay a chance,' Jean laughed. 'He's only just got back.'

Barclay smiled at them both. 'There'll be plenty of time,' he said.

THE END

Other titles in the
Linford Western Library:

THE DEVIL'S WORK

Paul Bedford

Marshal Rance Toller is locking up a pair of troublemakers when Angie Sutter, a homesteader from a nearby valley, arrives with the news that her husband was murdered that morning. Whilst Rance has qualms about heading out into the frozen wasteland, leaving only an ageing deputy to stand guard, he accompanies Angie to her cabin — to find not only Jacob Sutter's body, but also that of his neighbour, slain by the same weapon. Meanwhile, back at the jailhouse, the deputy is dead and the prisoners gone . . .

REBEL RAIDERS

John Dyson

A gang of former Confederate soldiers is robbing and killing its way across Kansas. Novice lawman Cass Clacy is sent out after them, but what chance does he have of outgunning such experienced fighters? When Sheriff Jim Clarke joins Cass in the chase, his main aim is a share of the reward. Together they penetrate deep into the heart of the Indian Nations, where Cass falls under the spell of the lovely Audrey — but can he save her from the clutches of the dangerous Josiah Baines?

THE COMANCHE FIGHTS AGAIN

D. M. Harrison

Mitch Bayfield, known as 'Broke', was kidnapped and raised as a Comanche. When, many years later, he looks for his kin, he finds himself unable to settle in either world and turns his back on them all. He is determined, however, to return and liberate Little Bluestem, another white captive. The two of them flee, with the Comanche hot on their trail — but they are about to tangle with a ruthless gang of bank robbers . . .

THE PRISONER OF GUN HILL

Owen G. Irons

When Luke Walsh falls for the beautiful Dee Dee Bright, he makes the biggest mistake of his young life. After she tricks him into killing the marshal of Tucson, Arizona, there is nothing for it but to take to the desert. But when his horse founders, he finds himself afoot and alone on the plain. Picked up by a passing wagon, he is set to work as slave labour in the Gun Hill gold mine — the remote outpost harbouring a nest of dangerous outlaws . . .